Easter Escapade
by

Kathi Daley

This book is dedicated to
Christina Kenison
and
the gang at the Winnemucca Animal
Rescue
for caring for and about the animals who
depend on them for a helping hand.

I want to thank the very talented Jessica Fischer for the cover art.

I so appreciate Bruce Curran, who is always ready and willing to answer my cyber questions, and Peggy Hyndman for helping sleuth out those pesky typos.

And, of course, thanks to the readers and bloggers in my life, who make doing what I do possible.

Thank you to Randy Ladenheim-Gil for the editing.

Special thanks to Sharon Guagliardo, Patty Liu, Pam Curran, and Nancy Farris for submitting recipes.

And finally I want to thank my sister Christy for always lending an ear and my husband Ken for allowing me time to write by taking care of everything else.

Books by Kathi Daley

Come for the murder, stay
for the romance.

Zoe Donovan Cozy Mystery:
Halloween Hijinks
The Trouble With Turkeys
Christmas Crazy
Cupid's Curse
Big Bunny Bump-off
Beach Blanket Barbie
Maui Madness
Derby Divas
Haunted Hamlet
Turkeys, Tuxes, and Tabbies
Christmas Cozy
Alaskan Alliance
Matrimony Meltdown
Soul Surrender
Heavenly Honeymoon
Hopscotch Homicide
Ghostly Graveyard
Santa Sleuth
Shamrock Shenanigans
Kitten Kaboodle
Costume Catastrophe

Candy Cane Caper
Holiday Hangover
Easter Escapade
Camp Carter – *July 2017*

Zimmerman Academy The New Normal
Ashton Falls Cozy Cookbook

Tj Jensen Paradise Lake Mysteries by Henery Press

Pumpkins in Paradise
Snowmen in Paradise
Bikinis in Paradise
Christmas in Paradise
Puppies in Paradise
Halloween in Paradise
Treasure in Paradise – *April 2017*
Fireworks in Paradise – *October 2017*

Whales and Tails Cozy Mystery:

Romeow and Juliet
The Mad Catter
Grimm's Furry Tail
Much Ado About Felines
Legend of Tabby Hollow
Cat of Christmas Past
A Tale of Two Tabbies
The Great Catsby

Count Catula
The Cat of Christmas Present
A Winter's Tail
The Taming of the Tabby – *June 2017*

Seacliff High Mystery:
The Secret
The Curse
The Relic
The Conspiracy
The Grudge
The Shadow – *June 2017*

Sand and Sea Hawaiian Mystery:
Murder at Dolphin Bay
Murder at Sunrise Beach
Murder at the Witching Hour
Murder at Christmas
Murder at Turtle Cove
Murder at Water's Edge – *May 2017*

Road to Christmas Romance:
Road to Christmas Past

Writer's Retreat Southern Mystery:

First Case – *May 2017*
Second Look – *July 2017*

Chapter 1

Thursday, April 13

The sun shining through the bedroom window gave evidence to the fact that it was going to be a sunny spring day. I glanced at my husband, Zak Zimmerman, who was snoring softly beside me before slipping quietly out of bed. I pulled off the large T-shirt I slept in before pulling on a pair of gray sweatpants, a black T-shirt, and a black-and-gold Ashton Falls Bulldogs sweatshirt. Then I pulled on a pair of warm socks and slipped my feet into a pair of worn Nikes. I motioned for the dogs to follow me as I went through the bedroom door and silently made my way through the silent house. It seemed everyone had decided to sleep in with both the public schools and Zimmerman Academy closed this week for spring break.

Once I arrived at the bottom of the stairs, I glanced down the long hallway. Zak had spent the previous day helping my best friends, Levi and Ellie Denton, move into our downstairs suite. The boathouse, which Zak and I owned and they lived in, was scheduled for a major remodel beginning next week. We were adding two bedrooms, another bathroom, and a new kitchen, which would involve the removal of one wall, requiring people, animals, and furnishings to be vacated from the property prior to the beginning of construction. Ellie was pregnant with her first child, a boy they were naming Eli. She was due to deliver at any moment, which meant the timing of the move was less than ideal. If the weather hadn't been a concern we might have waited, but in our snowy climate the building season was limited. Putting off such a large project even a couple of months wasn't an option if we wanted to have it completed before the start of the next snow season. Zak and I wanted Ellie to be as comfortable as possible, so we'd insisted that the newly married couple stay with us rather than in a motel while the renovation was underway.

Initially Levi and Ellie were hesitant to take us up on our offer. Ellie wasn't the sort to want to impose, but I pointed out that Zak's mansion had ten bedrooms while currently housing only four residents occupying three bedrooms, and staying with us would be a much more enjoyable experience than staying in an impersonal motel. Zak and me, as well as the two children who lived with us, Alex Bremmerton and Scooter Sherwood, all had bedrooms on the second floor, and we could offer the couple privacy at the end of the wing on the first floor. The suite had a sliding glass door leading out to the patio, providing them with a private entrance should they desire it.

Of course I should mention that in addition to the four human residents of our lakeside estate, there are also three dogs and three cats. And when you add in Levi and Ellie's two dogs and cat, the animals outnumbered the humans nine to six, but as far as our particular family is concerned, that's exactly the way it should be.

I quietly gathered all the household dogs and then scribbled a quick note for the others should they awake. I attached collars to the five canine members of the household and headed out into the crisp morning air. I jogged slowly along the sand so that my dog, Charlie, could keep up. He's the smallest of the dogs by far, half Tibetan terrier and half mystery dog, weighing in at just about twenty pounds. Zak's dog, Bella, a Newfoundland, is the largest, weighing in at more than one hundred and fifty pounds, while Scooter's lab, Digger, Ellie's German shepherd, Shep, and Levi's lab, Karloff, fill in the middle in relation to the size of the pack.

I smiled as I felt the warm sun on my back. We were lucky to have an early spring this year. I've witnessed many Aprils when the snow still covered the ground and the flowers didn't make an appearance until well in to June. This year we'd had early snow and then a long dry spell. The temperatures were unseasonably warm, melting what was left of the white stuff, so the only snow that remained was found high up on the mountain.

I slowed to a walk to give Charlie a rest. The water in the lake would be frigid, but the glassy surface, combined with the warm sunshine, had me thinking of the wakeboarding and sailing that would be just around the corner. I loved to ski and I loved winters in Ashton Falls, but the warmer days of summer couldn't come fast enough for me.

I was debating whether to turn around and head back to the house when I came across a pile of clothing on the beach, consisting of a pair of tennis shoes, a pair of jeans, a white long-sleeved T-shirt, and a blue sweatshirt with "Dolphin Bay Resort" written across the front. I looked out into the water and saw someone swimming toward shore towing what looked to be another person. As quickly as I could, despite the cold, I kicked off my shoes and socks and then stripped down to my bra and panties. I dove into the water to help her. I couldn't imagine what anyone would be doing swimming in the lake at this time of the year. Both the water and air temperature were only around fifty degrees, making for a chilly, even dangerous outing indeed.

"What's going on?" I asked the woman with dark hair, golden brown skin, and dark eyes.

"I was out taking a walk and saw something floating on the surface of the water. When I realized it was a person I swam out to help, but it was too late. Geez, this water is cold."

"Yeah, it really is." I glanced at the body, which was wearing black dress slacks and a light gray dress shirt under a life vest. Black leather shoes and black socks covered his feet, although he didn't have on an outer jacket or sweater of any type. I couldn't imagine what he was doing in the water. He certainly wasn't dressed for swimming. "We need to get back to shore before hypothermia sets in. I'll help you."

The woman and I each looped an arm beneath a shoulder of the man, who looked to have been in his mid-fifties and was obviously already dead and made our way to shore. He was vaguely familiar, but my mind, which was occupied with trying to keep me from freezing, couldn't quite pull up his identity. Luckily, the woman I was helping was in excellent shape and a better swimmer even than I was, so we made it to the beach before we both succumbed to the cold.

We both quickly pulled off our wet underthings and put on our dry clothing before either of us spoke. Finally she looked in my direction and introduced herself. "My name is Lani Pope. I'm visiting from Hawaii, staying in the cabin just down the way."

"Zoe Donovan-Zimmerman. I live down the beach in the other direction. These are Charlie, Bella, Digger, Shep, and Karloff," I introduced the dogs. "I have to say, you're quite a swimmer. Do you compete?"

"I did when I was in high school, but I don't anymore." Lani pulled her long black hair into a ponytail, twisted it to ring out the excess water, and knotted it at the back of her neck. "I'm a lifeguard. I'm used to making rescues, but not to diving into water quite this cold. I had no idea it would be this bad until I actually was in it."

"The water in the lake basically comes from snow runoff." I was still shivering, but now that I was dressed I was beginning to warm up. The higher the sun rose in the sky, the warmer it became. "We should call this in." I grabbed my phone from the pocket of my sweatpants and dialed Sheriff Salinger's cell number. It was still early, so I doubted he'd be in his office yet, but I knew he considered himself to always be on call and kept his cell handy.

"Donovan," he barked, obviously unhappy about being bothered so early in the morning. "This better be important."

"It is," I assured him as I glanced at the body lying on the sand. "I'm on the beach." I looked around. "I guess about halfway between my house and Hardaway Beach. I was out for a jog and came across a visitor who was attempting a rescue. The victim, a man who I would say is in his midfifties, didn't make it."

I heard Salinger groan and let out a long sigh. "Do you know who it is?"

"No, although he does look familiar."

"Okay. I'm on my way. Don't disturb the body in any way until I get there."

"Just hurry." I ended the call and returned the phone to my pocket. Then I looked toward Lani, who was staring at the body with a worried expression on her face. "Sheriff Salinger is on his way," I told her.

"You have the sheriff's home number?" Lani appeared surprised by this fact.

I nodded. "His cell."

"Are you friends?"

I rubbed my hands together in an attempt to warm them. "In a roundabout sort of way. We certainly didn't start off friends. In fact, we hated each other quite a lot in the beginning, but I have a knack for getting mixed up in murder mysteries and over time Salinger began to see the wisdom in letting me poke around. I guess you can say that after three years and twenty-some-odd murders, we've grown to appreciate each other."

Lani grinned. "I think we're going to be kindred spirits, Zoe. I too am known as something of an amateur sleuth, although being an amateur isn't something I aspire to."

"No?"

"I come from a cop family. My father and uncle are both retired from the Honolulu Police Department and all five of my older brothers are currently cops within the Hawaiian Islands. What I really want is to utilize my skills in an official capacity."

The woman had a look of fierce determination in her eyes that conveyed that one way or another she was going to make her dream a reality.

"I realize I just met you, but based on what I've just seen it seems to me you'd make a good cop. What's the problem?" I asked.

Lani sighed. "I may not be moving up the list due to my size, but to tell you the truth, I think my inability to make it into the police academy has more to do with my overprotective family. It's not easy being both female and petite when you have five big, burly brothers who look at you like a fragile flower in need of protection."

"No, I suppose it isn't."

Lani looked down at the body. "Do you know who he is?"

I frowned. "I'm not sure. I recognize him, but I'm having a hard time placing where I know him from."

"Do you think we should check his pockets? For ID?"

Salinger wouldn't like that and he'd told me not to disturb the body, but I needed something to do to keep my mind off the cold, so I bent down and began searching for the man's wallet. I found it in his back left pocket. I slid it out and opened it to reveal a soaking-wet stack of twenty-dollar bills, a credit card, and a Massachusetts driver's license that identified him as Charles Rossi.

My heart sank. "I just remembered where I know him," I said as I glanced up from the wallet to look at Lani. "He's a historian I met at my friend Ethan Carlton's home. Ethan's a history teacher at Zimmerman Academy, and they know each other somehow. Anyway, Charles Rossi was in the area to do research for a book he's writing about the history of this area."

Lani wrapped her arms around her body, I assumed in an attempt to warm herself. "I wonder what happened to him."

"I don't know. He doesn't appear to have any external injuries that would indicate he was dead before ending up in the lake, and he's wearing a life vest but fully clothed, so it doesn't appear he planned to take a swim. Besides, even a visitor would know it would be suicide to go for a swim this early in the year. He must have been pushed or fallen from a boat."

Lani looked out across the glassy lake. "It's a big lake. He could have been dumped anywhere, although you don't have currents to deal with like you do in the ocean."

"There hasn't been any wind. I'm guessing he entered the water not far from where you found him."

Lani turned and looked down the beach. "Do you mind if I use your phone to call my boyfriend? He must be wondering what happened to me."

"Yeah, no problem."

I handed my phone to Lani, who made her call. "Thanks," she said as she handed the phone back to me when she was finished. "I left my cell on the nightstand. Luke is on his way down the beach and he's is bringing a couple of blankets for us to wrap up in."

"Have you been at the lake long?" I asked after returning the phone to my pocket.

"Just a couple of days. We both have busy lives on Oahu but decided to carve out some quiet time before the summer tourist season hits. The cabin we're staying in is owned by Luke's uncle, who offered it to us for two weeks."

I watched as a tall man with blond hair and broad shoulders hurried toward us with blankets in his arms. He wore dark denim jeans and a sky-blue sweatshirt. He wasn't quite as tall as Zak, but his overall build and coloring, combined with the look of panicked concern on his face, reminded me a lot of him. I should probably call him as well.

Lani introduced me to Luke Austin after he'd handed a blanket to each of us. I excused myself to make my call while he fussed over Lani, likely in an attempt to ensure she was okay.

"Hey, it's me," I said when Zak answered the phone. I felt bad when I realized he'd still been asleep.

"Where are you?" he asked groggily.

I explained, and suddenly the grogginess in his voice was replaced with concern. He asked if I'd called Salinger, and when I assured him I had, he said he was on his way. If I knew Zak, and I did, he'd arrive within minutes with hot coffee all around. He was the most capable man on the planet. We'd been together for over three years and it still amazed me how he managed to see to every little detail, no matter the situation. I glanced at the tender way Luke was fussing over Lani, who looked annoyed. I smiled. I used to hate it when Zak fussed over me in just that way, so I could identify with what she was feeling. Zak used to treat me like a *fragile flower* too, making me feel weak and incapable, but as time had gone by and I'd realized it came from a place of love, I'd learned to appreciate what a wonderful man I had and how lucky I was he was mine.

Sure enough, Zak arrived with a large thermos full of coffee and five cups just about the time Salinger pulled up. Everyone introduced themselves while Salinger knelt down to examine the body.

"I'm guessing he was in the water at least a couple of hours. There doesn't appear to be any indication he was injured prior to entering the water, although we'll have a better idea about that after the medical examiner takes a look. His life jacket would have kept him afloat, so I doubt he drowned. I'm thinking the cause of death is going to be hypothermia."

I knelt down next to Salinger. "Yeah, that's what I thought as well. After I spoke to you I remembered who he was: a visiting historian Ethan introduced me to the other day. His name is Charles Rossi and he was here from Boston, doing research for a book he's writing."

Salinger stood up and faced Lani. "You find the body?"

"Yes. I was out for an early walk and saw him floating on the surface."

"How far out was he?"

Lani glanced out across the lake. "I guess maybe about three or four hundred yards. I wasn't even sure it was a person at first. I watched the water for a while before I realized it was a body and headed in. He was already gone. I was towing him in when Zoe came down the beach. She dove in and helped me."

"Was he face up or down when you found him?"

"Face down. I flipped him over just to make sure he was beyond needing CPR. When I realized he'd been gone for quite some time I began to tow him in."

"Lani is a lifeguard in Hawaii," I explained. "I imagine most people wouldn't have had the endurance to tow the body as far as she had in the frigid water."

"And your purpose for being in the area?" Salinger asked Lani.

"We're on vacation."

Salinger looked Lani up and down, as if she was a suspect, which annoyed me. I gave him a hard look. "Lani is a witness, not a suspect. And she's as soaking wet as I am. If you don't need us right now I'd love to head home to change into dry clothes, and I'm sure Lani would as well."

Salinger shrugged. "Okay. I know where to find you if I have additional questions." Then he turned to Lani. "If you'll give me a cell-phone number you can go as well."

I gave Lani my number and she gave me hers before we parted ways. I could tell she was curious about the who and why behind the man's death, so I arranged for her and Luke to have dinner with Zak and me that evening. I figure we could get to know one another a bit, and if Salinger had figured anything out by then, I could share that information with the spunky woman I was already thinking of as a friend.

Chapter 2

Back at the house I took a long, hot shower before dressing in a pair of faded jeans, a red T-shirt, and a dark blue sweatshirt. Then I put on thick socks and a new pair of running shoes and pulled my long, curly hair into a ponytail rather than taking the time to dry and style it, and headed downstairs, where I found the rest of the household sharing the breakfast I was sure Zak had made for them. I poured myself a large cup of coffee, added a splash of milk, and sat down between Ellie and Alex.

"It sounds like you had an exciting morning." Ellie was still in her pajamas, although she'd combed her long dark hair and secured it off her face with a barrette. She buttered a piece of sourdough toast.

Before answering, I took a sip of my coffee and glanced at the woman who looked like she was going to pop at any moment. "I'm not sure *exciting* is the best word, but I did meet a nice couple who are staying down the beach. They're visiting from Hawaii. Anyway, I'm sorry about Ethan's friend."

"I don't believe I had the chance to meet him," Ellie commented. "Were they close?"

"I don't know how long they knew each other, but they seemed close. I'm sure Ethan's going to be devastated."

"Any idea what happened?" Levi asked, pushing his thick, dark hair back from his forehead.

"It looked like he must have been pushed or fallen from a boat," I answered. "I'm sure Salinger will have more to say about it after the medical examiner has a chance to look over the body."

"Do you think Ethan knows?" Ellie asked.

I paused. "I'm not sure. I did tell Salinger the man was a friend of Ethan's, so I imagine he'll speak to him at some point today. I thought I'd go by Ethan's house after I check in at the Zoo." I'd referred to Zoe's Zoo, the wild and domestic animal rescue and rehabilitation shelter I owned and operated with the help of my assistant, Jeremy Fisher. I glanced at Zak, who was shoveling eggs into his mouth. "Are you and Levi going to finish moving the furniture into storage today?"

Zak nodded. "I spoke to the contractor and he said he can start the prep this weekend if the place is empty."

"This weekend is Easter," I reminded him.

He shrugged. "He didn't seem to mind. Not everyone celebrates the holiday."

I supposed Zak had a point. While I had a big family gathering planned for Sunday that included egg coloring with the kids and an egg hunt for my three-year-old sister Harper and Jeremy's daughter Morgan Rose, also three, it would be just a regular weekend to a lot of folks.

"Can I go over to Tucker's today?" Scooter asked.

"If it's okay with his aunt," I answered. "I can drop you there on my way into town." I glanced at Alex. "How about you? Do you have plans?"

"I'm going to stay here to help Ellie get Baby Eli's room ready. It won't be long until he's here."

Ellie smiled at Alex. I knew she really appreciated the girl's interest in making sure everything was ready for the newborn when he arrived. Alex was brilliant, though somewhat socially awkward with kids her own age, but she had a kind soul and a giving nature that made her a favorite among the adults in her life. When she first came to live with Zak and me she was shy and insecure. Her parents were archeologists who traveled the world chasing the next big find, so Alex had spent her childhood being shuffled around between boarding schools, summer camps, and nannies. Due to her advanced intelligence, she didn't really identify with kids her own age, creating a situation where she was isolated and alone much of the time. Since she'd moved in with us and begun attending classes at Zimmerman Academy, she was blossoming into a caring young woman with friends of all ages.

"Zak and I are going to take the couple we met this morning out to dinner tonight," I announced. "I thought maybe you all could just call for takeout."

"I'll cook something for Levi, me, and the kids," Ellie volunteered.

"Are you sure?" I asked. Ellie had owned her own restaurant and was by far the best cook among us, but she was also nine months pregnant. "I don't want you to tire yourself out."

"I like to cook. It's relaxing. I'll see what you have on hand, and I can send Levi to the store if I need anything."

"Okay, then make yourself at home." I glanced at Levi. "In fact, if you do end up going to the store grab four dozen eggs."

"Four dozen?"

"Easter eggs. I have the color pellets, but I need more eggs."

"Are you all set for Easter dinner?" Ellie asked.

I glanced at Zak.

"I bought everything I need the other day," Zak confirmed. "I figured I'd grab some fresh veggies on Saturday, which is when I plan to make the pies and rolls. I think we're good to go for right now."

I loved big family holidays and couldn't wait for the weekend to arrive. I just hoped the investigation into Charles Rossi's death, which I suspected I'd be involved in, didn't interfere with the laundry list of activities I had planned. I glanced at the log cabin clock on the wall. "Ethan should be up and about. I'm going to call him to make sure he's okay with me coming by." I glanced at Scooter. "Finish eating, then run up and brush your teeth and make sure Tucker's aunt knows you're coming."

"I will," Scooter assured me.

******

Jeremy pulled into the parking lot at Zoe's Zoo just ahead of me. When Zak had first bought the shelter for me, after I'd been fired by the county, I'd worked it like a full-time job, but now that I was married and had two children I was responsible for, I'd turned the daily operations over to Jeremy and served in more of a supervisory capacity.

"Beautiful day," Jeremy greeted me as I slipped out of the new dark green convertible Zak had bought me a few weeks earlier, when it became evident we really were going to have the early spring that had been predicted.

"It really is. I saw on the weather report that the high temperature is supposed to be in the mid-sixties all weeks."

"I'm definitely ready for a little warmth and sunshine."

Jeremy opened the front door of the shelter and motioned for me to precede him inside.

"I can't stay long," I said. "I'm afraid a friend of Ethan's who's been visiting from the East Coast was found dead in the lake this morning. I'm heading over to his place after I finish here."

"Dead?" Jeremy asked, surprise evident on his face.

I *had* announced the fact that a man was dead in a manner that was more casual than warranted. Ever since I'd become involved in helping Salinger deal with the murder spree we seemed to be having the past few years, I'd developed something of a cavalier attitude toward death that wasn't a good thing. To be honest, it was beginning to worry me quite a lot that I no longer felt a sense of horror when I came across the remains of a man or woman who had suffered an untimely death.

"The man's name was Charles Rossi. He was in town doing research for a book. I'm not sure whether he was staying with Ethan, and I don't know exactly how close they were, but Mr. Rossi was found fully clothed floating on the surface of the lake early this morning by another visitor to the area, a lifeguard named Lani Pope." I spoke slowly and softly, in a tone I hoped communicated my sorrow. I needed to work on that if I didn't want to come off sounding callous.

Jeremy ran a hand though his long dark hair. "Wow. Ethan introduced him to me not long ago. He grew up in the same town in the south where my mother did, which led to a conversation about how much the place had changed in the past forty years. Do you know how he ended up in the water?"

"He was wearing a life vest, but I've been assuming he was pushed from a boat, which would indicate to me, at least, that he was murdered. It doesn't make sense that he decided to take a frigid swim and didn't even bother to take off his shoes." I walked down the hallway with Jeremy following behind me. I opened the door to my office and went inside.

"I'm not sure if this is relevant, but I saw him last night."

I turned back to Jeremy. "Last night? Where?"

"He was at the new Italian place down by the wharf. I'm pretty sure it's called Isabella's. Jessica and I were there for our weekly date night and I saw him having dinner with another man."

"What time was that?"

"Around six-thirty."

"Did you speak to them?"

"No. They were in the middle of a conversation and I didn't want to interrupt."

"This other man—what did he look like?"

Jeremy paused as he considered my question. "He looked to be tall, although he was sitting down, so I'm not sure of his actual height. Probably taller than Ethan's friend by several inches at least. He was fit-looking, with muscular arms and a thick neck. He had short, light-colored hair with streaks of gray."

"Did you notice what the men were wearing?"

"Isabella's is a fairly nice eatery, so both men were wearing dress shirts and jackets, but I don't think either of them had on ties. Why are you interested in what they wore?"

"When Mr. Rossi's body was found this morning he was wearing black dress pants, a gray dress shirt, black socks, and black dress shoes. He also wore a life vest, but he didn't have on a jacket."

"Sounds like what he had on last night minus the jacket," Jeremy confirmed. "If he wanted to wear a life vest it may not have fit over it."

"Good point."

I paused to consider the situation. Salinger had said Rossi had only been in the water a few hours, which meant he must have been out or at least occupied all night. It didn't sound like he'd slept during the time between his dinner at Isabella's and his entry into the lake. Unless, of course, he'd slept in his clothes or dressed early this morning in the same clothes he'd worn the night before, which didn't seem likely.

"I don't suppose you overheard what the men were discussing?"

"No. We passed the table while being seated, but our table was across the restaurant."

"Were they still there when you left?"

Jeremy shook his head. "No, they were gone. I didn't see them leave, but when we passed back through the restaurant on our way out a man and woman were sitting at their table. Maybe Ethan knows who the other man is."

"I'll ask him. I don't know enough to be certain how Charles Rossi ended up in the lake, but I have to believe it was foul play. If he'd simply fallen overboard whoever he was with could have helped him back into the boat, and if he was alone we should find an empty boat floating around somewhere."

"Most boats, especially rentals, are equipped with a kill switch, so if he'd been alone and fell overboard somehow the boat would have been found in the same vicinity as the body. Like you, I think he must have been pushed."

I made a mental note to ask Ethan about the tall man and to stop in at the restaurant to see if anyone there might know who he was. If he'd been the one to make the reservation or paid with a credit card they could very well supply a name.

******

Ethan's house looked exactly like you'd expect the home of a single male history professor who'd traveled the world would. The walls were lined with shelves that held books, art, and artifacts. The entire house was decorated in tones of brown and beige, and the furniture had been selected for comfort rather than aesthetic appeal. Ethan's office featured a huge desk that was surrounded by file cabinets. The only softness to the room was a large, fluffy white cat who watched us from the sofa.

I'd briefly filled Ethan in on the fate of his friend when I'd called earlier, so he was aware of what I was there to discuss. It seemed that if we were going to understand who might have killed Charles Rossi—and I did suspect he'd been murdered—we needed to understand what sort of motive might have emerged from the research he was doing about the area, which seemed to be the most likely reason for it.

I sat down on one of the leather chairs across from Ethan's desk while he pulled a stack of books from the corner. He opened the first book and began thumbing through it. He located what he was looking for, then passed it across to me.

"What am I looking at?" I asked. The photo on the page was in black and white and looked very old.

"The two men in the photo lived here when Ashton Falls was still Devil's Den," Ethan began.

Devil's Den had been an active mining camp from the 1880s until the gold dried up in the mid-1940s. By the time Ashton Montgomery, a multimillionaire and my great-grandfather on my mother's side, bought the land in the 1950s, the area was all but deserted. He'd leveled many of the old buildings and built Ashton Falls as sort of a touristy tribute to himself.

"The man on the left is Warren Goldberg," Ethan continued.

I remembered Warren Goldberg from a treasure hunt Ethan, I, and a few others had participated in a couple of years ago. We'd been trying to find the gold left to a man who, at the time, was in the hospital, dying. Goldberg had come to Ashton Falls in 1908. Prior to settling in Devil's Den, he'd owned a sailing vessel he'd sold to fund his journey west. He'd brought with him a masthead carved to resemble his dead fiancée, one of the clues we were seeking. Goldberg eventually had sold the masthead to raise the funds to open the area's first medical clinic.

"And the other man?" I asked.

"Charles's grandfather: Antonio Rossi. Antonio Rossi and Warren Goldberg had been friends before he headed west. The photo was taken some time between 1915 and 1918."

I looked at the photo. There didn't appear to be a date anywhere in sight. "How do you know that?" I asked.

"Because Charles told me that Antonio made the trip west to visit his old friend in 1915, and according to what Charles had been able to uncover, he stayed here for three years."

I sat back in my chair and tried to remember everything I'd learned about that time period. I hadn't paid much attention when we'd studied local history in school, but I'd been involved in two different treasure hunts relating to local history: the search for Dr. Ozwald's gold and the search for Isaac Wainwright's stone. There are those who might think being involved in two treasure hunts in one lifetime was quite a lot, but the reality was that Ashton Falls had been rich with gold and multiple legends about buried treasure existed to this day.

"I'm following so far. What was Mr. Rossi here to find out? I thought he was doing research for a book. Was he looking for a buried treasure as well?"

"Sort of."

Okay, that piqued my interest. "Sort of?"

"Charles's father died six months ago. Charles was an only child, so it was left to him to dispose of his father's property. While he was sorting through some boxes in the attic of the old man's home he came across his grandfather's journal, including entries dating between 1915 and 1918, and one of them had a detailed report of Antonio's time in Devil's Den. Included in the journal was a mention of a man named Peter Romanov, a very distant relation to Tsar Nicholas II of Russia. Peter claimed to have smuggled important documents, jewels, and priceless artifacts out of Russia in 1915 after World War I upset the balance of power and things began to fall apart in Europe. He headed east and arrived in the States on the West

Coast via a ship Charles believed landed somewhere along the Oregon coast. Charles didn't have all the details, but it seemed that after living there for a short time, Peter decided he would prefer the culturally advanced East Coast, so he packed up his possessions and headed east. He was on his way to Boston when he became ill. He stopped in Devil's Den to recuperate, but in the end he died. On his deathbed he told Antonio where he had hidden the items he had taken out of Russia and asked him to ensure that the items were returned to the tsar after the war."

"But the tsar was forced to abdicate and eventually was executed."

"Exactly. Apparently Antonio decided to go home in early 1918. According to the journal Charles found, his grandfather didn't want to have the responsibility of traveling with such valuable items, so he left them behind, planning to return for them at some later date, when the world was once again stable and he could return the items to their rightful owner."

I supposed that made sense. "And did he ever come back for the treasure?"

"No. He died in an accident shortly after returning home. As far as Charles knew, his grandfather never told anyone about the treasure Peter Romanov had entrusted to him or where to find it. At least no one ever spoke of it. He said he would never have known of its existence if he hadn't read about it in the journal."

I paused as I let everything sink in. This was really interesting. A lot more interesting, in fact, than anything I could have imagined when I'd come to Ethan to ask about a history professor who might have been murdered.

"I want to be sure I have this straight. In response to changes in the political climate, Peter Romanov, some sort of distant relation of the tsar of Russia, took important documents, gems, and artifacts out of the country and brought them to the United States, where he hid them in Devil's Den after becoming ill while traveling. On his deathbed he told Charles Rossi's grandfather where he'd hidden the loot and asked him to return it to the tsar when the war was over. While the war was still in progress, Antonio Rossi decided to go home. The treasure remained hidden in what I assume he believed to be a safe place, so rather than risk traveling with it, he left it behind, planning to return for it after the war had run its course. He died before he could do that. Rossi believed that, while his grandfather wrote about the treasure in his journal, he never told anyone where it had been hidden in Devil's Den."

"That's it in a nutshell."

"So Charles Rossi came to Ashton Falls now to look for the treasure under the cover of doing research for a book."

"I believe so; however..."

I waited for Ethan to finish his thought. "However...?" I prompted him.

"I spoke to Charles about it on several occasions and was left with the impression there was something more going on. Something he didn't want to say. Although I invited him to stay here with me, he said he preferred to stay in a motel. And while we talked at length about the journal and the treasure that may still be hidden somewhere, he never gave me the opportunity to look at the journal. In fact, on the one occasion when I mentioned I'd love to see it he was very noncommittal."

"Maybe he thought you were going to steal his treasure."

"I don't think it was that. I mean, if he were worried about that why bring it up to me in the first place? He could simply have said he was here on vacation and I wouldn't have known differently."

I sat back and considered the situation. I had to admit I was more than a little intrigued. "Do you know where the journal is? Maybe if we can find out what he was up to we can figure out who might have killed him."

Ethan shook his head. "After you informed me that Charles was dead I went to his motel room. The door was unlocked, so I let myself in, only to find that it had been ransacked. I looked in the closet, under the mattress, and through all the drawers, but I didn't find the journal, so I'm assuming whoever killed Charles was successful in finding it. I'm afraid it may already be in the hands of the murderer."

"Maybe. But then again, if Rossi knew someone else was interested in the same thing he was it would have made sense for him to have hidden the journal rather than just leaving it in his motel room. Let's face it: motel rooms aren't all that secure. Did he visit you here often?"

Ethan narrowed his eyes. "You think he hid it in my house?"

"It would have been the smart thing to do."

"He did pop in for at least a few minutes almost every day," Ethan admitted.

"And when he was here? Where did he spend his time?"

Ethan's eyes lit up. "In the library."

Ethan's library was large, with floor-to-ceiling bookshelves on every wall. He hadn't accompanied Rossi into the library on most occasions, so he had no idea where he would have hidden the journal. It could be shelved among the other books or hidden at the back of a shelf. If he'd planned ahead it could even have been placed within a book with a false middle. As I looked at the huge task before us, I realized that even if we eventually found the book it would most likely take hours to do so. Still, it was the only lead we had.

As we looked, I asked Ethan if he knew who Rossi had dined with the night before. I described him based on what Jeremy had told me, but Ethan said he didn't sound familiar. I'd called Isabella's at eleven-thirty, when the restaurant opened for lunch, and asked in what name the reservation had been made. There was a different host working today, but this one checked and found a reservation at six o'clock the previous night in Rossi's name, and Rossi had also been the one to pay. I asked if last night's host would be in later and was told he would be in for the dinner shift at five-thirty. It wouldn't hurt to stop by to speak to him, just in case he'd happened to overhear the name of Rossi's companion.

Chapter 3

Zak and I decided to take Luke and Lani to the Wharf that evening. An upscale restaurant overlooking the lake, it served a delicious selection of steaks and seafood. Though my afternoon with Ethan had been one of the most fascinating I'd experienced for quite some time, I was looking forward to getting to know the couple from Hawaii.

"So you never found the journal?" Lani asked after I had recapped the details of my search with Ethan.

"Not yet," I answered, "but we plan to keep looking. The problem is that Ethan has thousands of books. The first thing we did was make a quick scan of the shelves to see if we could spot it, but once we realized Rossi probably hadn't left it sitting out in such an obvious way, we decided we needed to handle and open every book. It's going to take forever, but right now the possibility that the journal is somewhere in the library is the only idea we have."

"That sounds like a lot of work for a maybe," Lani commented. "Have you searched Rossi's motel room?"

I shook my head. "It was tossed. If the journal was on his person or in his room, whoever killed him most likely has it."

Lani's eyes shone with curiosity as we discussed the events of the afternoon. I could see that, like me, she had an active mind and the innate need to be involved in the solution to whatever problem might present itself.

"If you don't think your friend would mind, Luke and I would be happy to go with you tomorrow to help you look," Lani offered.

I noticed she hadn't asked Luke before volunteering him for the project, though she did glance at him after making the offer and smiled when he nodded.

"I think it'll be fine with Ethan and we could use the help." I turned to Zak. "Did you and Levi finish moving everything today? Would you be able to help us as well?"

Zak wiped his mouth on a napkin before replying. "I need to meet with the contractor first thing in the morning, but then I'm all yours."

I glanced back at Lani. "I'll call Ethan in the morning just to make certain he doesn't have any reservations about having extra help, but as long as he's cool with it, Zak and I will pick you up after he finishes with the contractor. I can text you to confirm a time after I speak to Ethan."

Lani smiled. "That sounds good. This whole thing has me intrigued. The idea that there are artifacts belonging to the Russian royal family hidden on United States soil is mind-boggling."

"It's possible the treasure was found years ago, even assuming the whole story isn't just some intriguing legend, but the idea of finding such a stash gives me chills up and down my arms too. Having said that, I'm not sure finding the treasure, if it's still there to find, will help us figure out who killed Rossi."

Lani took on a look of contemplation before responding. "It seems the search for something so valuable would serve as a motive for murder if Rossi had told others his real reason for being in Ashton Falls. If no one but your friend knew why he was really here I'm not sure how he would have attracted the attention of anyone who was looking to steal the treasure."

"That's true. I've been operating on the assumption that Rossi maintained his cover story of working on a book with everyone other than Ethan, but if he informed others of his true purpose I'd say that's probably what got him killed. My assistant, Jeremy, saw Rossi having dinner last night with a tall man with gray hair, but so far I haven't been able to find out who he was or what their relationship might have been."

"Did you ask at the restaurant where they dined?" Lani asked.

"Yes, but the reservation was under Rossi's name and he was the one who paid. When I spoke with the dinner host he did say the other man was at least six foot four, so I'm thinking he would definitely stand out. I'm going to continue to ask around. The two of them may have been seen together at other times."

Our conversation paused as the waiter took away our salad plates and then brought our entrées. I'd ordered the lobster and Zak a steak, while Luke and Lani both chose the swordfish. The restaurant was known for its fresh seafood, but I assumed Luke and Lani were used to fish caught the same day it was served. I was a little worried they would find it lacking, but they both said it was delicious and I chose to believe them.

"So tell us about Hawaii," I said after we'd all settled into our meals. "Zak and I visited Maui two years ago and I loved every minute of our stay." I paused. "Well, almost every minute. There was a murder while we were there and we got pulled into it, and there were a few hairy moments along the way."

"You were involved in a murder?" Lani asked, surprise evident in her voice.

"Zak and I were invited to a luau at the home of Zak's friend's parents. When the pig was unveiled it turned out that wasn't what was in the pit; it was Keoke's sister's fiancé, Anton."

Lani gasped. "I remember when that happened. My oldest brother is a member of Maui PD and my second brother works for HPD. I seem to remember it was HPD who responded when the killer was identified. That was a really high-profile case. I can't believe you were involved."

"It wasn't by choice." I paused. "Okay, maybe we didn't *have* to investigate just because we found the body, but I felt like there was some sort of amateur sleuth code that required me to finish whatever fate had put me in the middle of."

Zak and Luke both groaned, while Lani enthusiastically said she totally agreed.

"Being a lifeguard must be interesting," Zak said in a lame attempt to change the subject. While he always supported me, he wasn't a huge fan of my sleuthing hobby. I had a feeling Luke felt the same way about Lani's tendency to get involved.

"Honestly, being a lifeguard can be exciting and rewarding, but it can also be boring at times. I work at a resort where the water safety officers are assigned to the surfing beach, the family beach, or the family pool. I adore working the surfing beach, tolerate the family beach, and absolutely abhor the family pool. Still, as jobs go, it isn't bad. I get to spend my days outdoors and my uniform is a bathing suit. It isn't my dream job, but it'll do until HPD realizes my value and hires me." Lani set her fork aside and took a sip of her wine, then turned to Zak. "I understand you're in to computers."

"I dabble," Zak answered.

"Zak does more than dabble," I couldn't help but brag. "He made his first million in his garage before he was nineteen."

"Wait," Luke said, glancing at Zak. "You're *that* Zak Zimmerman?"

Zak shrugged. "If you mean am I the Zak Zimmerman who owns Zimmerman Enterprises, then, yeah."

Luke looked impressed. More than impressed, he looked amazed.

"You know who Zak is?" Lani asked Luke.

"Sure. Anyone in finance does. It isn't polite to discuss money at the dinner table, but suffice it to say that Zak is world-renowned for his work. He's not just a software developer; he's *the* software developer."

I grinned at Zak. Suddenly I couldn't wait to get him home. Listening to other people brag on him was kind of sexy. Not that I wasn't well aware of how absolutely fantastic he was, but since we'd been a married couple, with obligations and everyday lives, at times I did forget that Zak was a celebrity to much of the world, or at least the part of the world that knew about computers.

Zak discussed computers with Luke for a bit and then he asked Luke about his horses. I think it embarrassed him to have everyone gushing over him. Zak is a modest guy who doesn't like to parade around his wealth and intellect like some sort of prima donna. That's one of the things I love most about him. He's rich and gorgeous, with an IQ that's off the charts, but he's also a regular guy who does the laundry and grocery shopping while also running a software business and a private school. The very best thing about Zak was that no matter how busy he was he found time to be the perfect husband to me and an awesome dad to Alex and Scooter too.

By the time we'd had dessert I was certain I was going to enjoy sleuthing alongside Luke and Lani. They were smart and funny and seemed to have amassed a sleuthing history almost as impressive as mine. Okay, maybe not *quite* as impressive, I bragged silently to myself, but I'd been at it longer. Given time, I was certain they'd catch up.

We dropped them back at their cabin and headed home. It wasn't all that late, so I thought I'd call Ethan then so we could settle things and not have to waste time making plans in the morning. When we walked into the house Levi, Ellie, Scooter, Alex, and all the animals were watching a movie.

"How'd it go?" Ellie asked.

"Good," I said casually. I sort of felt bad that we hadn't invited Levi and Ellie to come with us instead of leaving them home to babysit, but I'd wanted to get to know Luke and Lani, and if we'd invited my best friends in the whole world I was afraid the visitors from Hawaii would feel uncomfortable. "How did things go here?"

"Good," Ellie replied.

"I'm going upstairs to change and call Ethan, but then I'll be back down to fill you in," I said.

Ellie smiled but didn't respond, and Levi hadn't even looked up from the movie.

Upstairs, I changed into comfortable sweats and washed the makeup off my face. I thought Zak would follow me up to change as well, but he'd sat down next to Scooter and started watching the movie. It was just as well. Chances were if Zak had joined me I would have been distracted by my recently ignited passion for the man I'd married and never would have gotten around to calling Ethan.

I took out my cell and sat down on the edge of my bed. Zak may not have followed me upstairs, but Charlie had. He jumped up onto the bed and put his head in my lap. I think he might be feeling just a tiny bit territorial with the extra dogs in the house. I dialed Ethan's number and waited for him to pick up. If he didn't, I was prepared to leave a message.

"Hey, Zoe, what's up?" Ethan said as soon as he answered. One of the advantages of caller ID was that you knew who was calling you before you answered.

"I wanted to talk to you about tomorrow. Remember the woman I told you about who found Charles Rossi's body?"

"The lifeguard from Hawaii?"

"Yes. Zak and I had dinner with Lani and her boyfriend tonight and both of them volunteered to come with Zak and me to help us look for the journal. I wanted to check with you to make sure that was okay."

Ethan didn't answer right away.

"I know I just met them," I continued, "but my sense is that they're trustworthy. Lani is a lifeguard who wants to be a cop and Luke is a retired stockbroker who now owns a horse ranch. They've been involved in solving crimes back home and I have a feeling they might be able to help us with this situation."

"Have you spoken to Salinger since this morning?" Ethan asked.

"No. I haven't had the chance. Did you learn something new?"

"Charles was hit on the head. Salinger said it's inconclusive whether he was hit by another person or hit his head on the way into the water. What he was sure of was that Charles died from drowning rather than hypothermia. Salinger suspects he was knocked out and then pushed face-first into the water."

I did remember Lani saying Rossi was face down in the water when she found him. "I didn't see any blood or notice a wound."

"According to the medical examiner it was so cold in the water that his blood had stopped flowing. The wound was small and hidden by his hair. Salinger said it might have caused him to temporarily pass out, but it wouldn't have killed him if he hadn't been tossed into the lake."

"Wow. I'm not sure whether that changes things, but it's a new twist. It's odd that Rossi had on a life vest."

"I'm not sure whether Charles was a good swimmer, but Salinger thinks he probably wasn't and therefore was uncomfortable in the boat. He might have donned the life vest for added security while traveling on the lake. Something happened during the excursion, which Salinger believes he initially engaged in voluntarily, and then was hit over the head and thrown overboard. Salinger suspects the killer panicked and didn't think to remove the life vest before pushing him out of the boat. Of course that's just a theory. There's no way to know for certain what occurred unless we find the killer or a witness."

I pondered the idea. "I guess Salinger's theory makes sense."

Ethan cleared his throat before he continued. "There's more. Salinger thinks the timeline is off. It now appears Charles died just an hour or so before you found him."

Okay, that was surprising. What was the man doing out on the lake at six o'clock in the morning?

"Given the timeline," Ethan continued, "do you think your new friend is actually the one who killed him?"

"Lani? No. Why would you say that?"

Ethan didn't answer, but I thought he must be sorting things out in his own mind. "I don't know," he finally said. "I guess I'm just tired and looking for answers. The alteration in the timeline has me imagining all sorts of strange scenarios."

"Lani entered the water from the beach. I know that because she'd left her clothes in the sand. And when I came across her, she was swimming toward land towing Rossi's body to the shore. The timing might be off from what we originally believed, but I feel certain she went into the water to try to save him, as she said. I know I just met her, but my intuition tells me we can trust her."

"If you have a good feeling about her I guess it's okay if she comes with you tomorrow. But you might want to have Zak run a quick check on both of them," Ethan suggested. "Just to be sure."

"Okay. I'll ask him about it after he finishes with the movie he's watching with the kids. Zak has to meet the contractor in the morning, but I anticipate we should get to your place by ten or ten-thirty. I'll call before we head over."

I hung up, called Charlie, and then headed downstairs. My gut told me Luke and Lani were on the up-and-up, but if it would assuage Ethan's concern it couldn't hurt to have Zak do a quick look-see to confirm they really were who they'd told us they were. There were times I felt like a voyeur, snooping around in other people's lives, but with Google and social media, everyone's life was pretty much an open book anyway.

"Did you get hold of Ethan?" Zak asked. He was sitting on the sofa next to Scooter, whose head was resting against Zak's shoulder.

I nodded. "He's okay with Luke and Lani coming with us tomorrow, but he wants you to take a quick peek first, just to be sure they are who they say."

"You're going somewhere with Luke and Lani tomorrow?" Ellie asked.

"To Ethan's, to search through thousands of books, looking for a journal that may not even be hidden in his library. You can come too if you want, but I have a feeling it's going to be boring as well as tiring."

"I don't suppose I'd be much help given my condition, and Alex and I need to work on Eli's temporary room, but I'd like to meet them. Why don't you invite them to dinner? I'll cook something yummy."

I hesitated for just a minute before I answered. I could see Ellie was feeling left out and wanted to be included, but I didn't want her tiring herself. "I'd like you and Levi to meet Luke and Lani and I think inviting them over is a good idea, but I don't want you to overdo. We could just get takeout."

"I won't overdo," Ellie promised.

"I'll help her," Alex volunteered.

"Okay, if you're sure. But if you find you're worn out by the end of the day text me and I'll pick something up on the way home."

As soon as the movie was over, Zak went into his office to do the background check on Luke and Lani, Levi and Ellie went to bed, and I followed Alex and Scooter upstairs to tuck them in. Okay, maybe tucking in twelve-year-olds wasn't necessary, and I didn't get around to it every night, but I wanted to make sure both of these amazing kids knew that even though their parents weren't around to have day-to-day relationships with them at the moment, they were loved and wanted by Zak and me.

"Did you have fun with Ellie today?" I asked Alex after she slid under the covers.

"I really did. Did she tell you what Eli's middle name is going to be?"

I paused. "I don't think they'd decided the last time we spoke about it. Did they decide?"

Alex grinned and nodded.

"Do you know what it is?"

Alex nodded again.

"Are you going to tell me?"

Alex shook her head. "No. I'll let Ellie tell you."

I kissed Alex on the forehead, tucked the covers around her, turned off the light, and closed the door. Then I went to Scooter's room and repeated the routine, although we chatted about lizards rather than baby names. There'd been a time just a few months ago that Zak and I had thought Scooter might disappear from our everyday lives. His father had gotten a new job and an even newer fiancée and thought he would like to try being a real father to Scooter again. He'd taken his son to Los Angeles over winter break, but by the time the visit came to an end he'd decided there might not be room in his life for his energetic son after all.

I felt bad for Scooter, but he hadn't wanted to move anyway, so perhaps things had worked out for the best.

After both kids were tucked in, the animals settled, and the lights all turned off, I returned to our room. I could hear Zak in the adjoining bathroom brushing his teeth. I snuggled Charlie in my arms after climbing into bed to wait for him. He must not have found anything alarming to have completed his search so quickly.

Zak was a conscientious guy but, like me, he tended to trust his gut feeling more than anything else. I could tell that he'd believed Luke and Lani were exactly who they seemed and was just going through the motions of the background check to appease Ethan.

"So?" I asked when he came into the bedroom.

"Everything I found showed they're who they said they were. I think we can trust them."

I let out a breath. "Good, because I really like them. I'm afraid, though, that Ellie might be a tiny bit jealous of the time we're spending with them."

Zak pulled me into his arms and settled me against his naked chest. "I think Ellie is feeling emotional in general. I'm sure she must be uncomfortable physically, and even though she wants to have a larger place to live, it's hard to have your whole life disrupted just as you're about to give birth. I'm sure she knows she's your best friend and Lani can't touch that, but it might be nice to reinforce it with some gesture."

"A gesture? What sort of a gesture?"

Zak caressed my hair. I shivered as his hand trailed down my arm. "If Luke and Lani do come to dinner tomorrow night it might be nice to play up the best-friend thing. Let Ellie know how much she means to you."

I climbed up on top of Zak and looked down into his deep blue eyes. I leaned forward so my lips were just barely touching his. "I can do that, but first I think I should show you how much *you* mean to me."

"Yeah?" I could feel Zak's smile against my lips.

"Yeah." I leaned forward the rest of the way and captured Zak's lips as the rest of the world faded away.

Chapter 4

Friday, April 14

I woke the next morning to a beautiful sunny day. There was something about the promise of spring after a long, cold winter that made my heart sing with the realization that summer was just around the corner. Zak had already left the room, so I slipped out of bed and plodded into our bathroom. I took a quick shower, then dressed in soft blue jeans, a bright yellow T-shirt, and a white hoodie. I slipped tennis shoes onto my feet and headed downstairs. It seemed I was the last to rise; the rest of the family was sitting around the table eating pancakes. I smiled at the feeling of family and community as everyone shared the first meal of the day.

"Morning, everyone," I greeted the gang as I poured myself a cup of coffee. I grabbed a plate from the cupboard, then sat down at the table. "Is Ellie still sleeping?"

"Yeah. She had a rough night," Levi answered. "I'm afraid these past couple of weeks have been tough on her."

"I can understand that. I bet she's pretty uncomfortable. Things will be better after Eli gets here."

"I hope so," Levi said. "I figured by the time we got to this point in the pregnancy she'd be superexcited that her due date was finally here, but instead of being excited she seems tired, depressed, and sort of moody."

I placed a hand over Levi's arm. "I'm sure she is excited, but I bet she's equally scared and most likely impatient. Just be there for her. Eli will be here before you know it."

Levi squeezed my hand and smiled at me.

Zak leaned over and kissed me on the cheek before pushing back his chair and getting up. "Sorry to eat and run, but I need to head over to meet the contractor. I'm hoping it won't take more than a couple of hours."

"Can you drop me off at Tucker's?" Scooter asked Zak. "His aunt knows I'm coming."

"If you hurry. I don't want to keep the contractor waiting."

Scooter jumped up and ran up the stairs.

"I have some errands to run," Levi said as he carried his plate to the sink. "I want to get an early start so I can get back here at a decent time. I'll see you all later," he added, heading down the hall.

I looked at Alex. "Are you still planning to help Ellie?"

"Yes. We're going to work on Baby Eli's room and then I'm going to help her make dinner. I think we're making lasagna."

"That sounds good. Ellie's lasagna is the best I've ever eaten."

"It really is. I think I'll go clean my room before I get too far into the day and forget all about it."

I wasn't worried about Alex forgetting to clean her room. She was the most mature, responsible, and conscientious twelve-year-old on the planet. I couldn't help but smile as I watched her take her plate to the sink.

Once everyone had gone and I was sitting alone at the large table I felt sort of deserted, although in fairness I was the one who'd slept in, so I couldn't blame anyone but myself for the fact that I was eating a solitary breakfast. I took two pancakes off the platter that had been set in the center of the table and poured syrup over the top. I carried the plate out onto the back deck and sat in the sunshine while I looked out over the lake and enjoyed the perfection of the moment. I had a feeling it was going to be a hectic day, followed by a hectic weekend, so having a few minutes of solitude was probably just what I needed to start the day.

I thought about the man whose body Lani had found in the lake the previous morning. The tsar's treasure could certainly serve as a motive for murder, but the method the killer had used seemed odd to me. I couldn't think of a single reason why anyone would be in a boat on the lake when the temperature couldn't have been more than thirty degrees at six o'clock in the morning. Sure, there were fishermen who went out that early even on frigid spring mornings, but the way Rossi was dressed didn't scream *fishing expedition* to me.

Still, the fishing angle was something to consider. There would have been fishing boats on the water by that time in the morning. Maybe someone had seen something. It was unlikely I'd be able to figure out the whole thing without gathering additional information, so I made a mental note to ask around at the marina, then turned my thoughts to the weekend and the half-dozen chores I still needed to tend to before everyone arrived on Easter.

I finished eating and texted Lani to set up a time for us to pick them up. Then I called Ethan, assured him that Zak had run the background check on Luke and Lani, and confirmed our visit. My last call was to Salinger. "Have there been any new developments in the Rossi case?" I asked as soon as he picked up his phone.

I heard Salinger clear his throat before he began to speak. "Actually, there has been. In fact, I was planning to call you a little later. It turns out the man staying in the motel room next to Rossi's heard loud noises coming from there the evening before Ms. Pope and you stumbled onto the body. He said he spotted a tall man with broad shoulders wearing a dark-colored hoodie and pants come to Rossi's door at around nine. He could hear the men arguing, although at the time he just figured they were drunk and being obnoxious and turned up his television rather than listening. There was a lot of crashing going on and he was thinking of calling my office to complain, but then he heard Rossi's door open, the man left, and the noise stopped, so he didn't bother."

"The guy never stopped to consider that maybe the guest in the next room was in trouble?" I asked incredulously.

"No. The man next door was angry about the noise but wasn't worried that something bad was going on. After I showed up and told him the man in the room next to him had most likely been murdered he seemed to feel bad about not reporting the fight."

I paused to gather my thoughts. If the man who'd seemingly trashed the room was there at nine, what had occurred between then and six the next morning, when Rossi's body ended up in the lake? "Did the guy in the next room see whether Rossi left the motel with the man he'd been arguing with?"

"He said he left alone. He took a sleeping pill and went to bed shortly after, so he didn't see or hear anything else."

"How about other visitors staying in the motel?" I asked.

"It's the off season, so the place is pretty empty. There was a young couple two doors down who stayed the night but left early the next morning. They paid cash and the desk clerk claims not to have any contact information or even a name for them. I got a pretty bad description of the man who checked in and the car, but the clerk didn't take down the license plate, so chances are that lead will be a dead end. There was one other man staying at the other end of the motel. He said he was out until eleven, which would have been after the man who visited Rossi left, and he didn't see or hear anything."

"That's it? There were only four rooms rented out that night?"

"If the desk clerk is to be believed."

"What about the clerk? Did he hear or see anything?"

"He says no. I asked to see the cash receipts for that night and it looked like the clerk accepted payment for five rooms rather than four. I asked him about it and he said he must have overcharged someone."

"Sounds suspect," I commented.

"I agree. I'm going to continue to ask around, but I have a feeling that finding a witness at the motel is going to be a dead end. I don't suppose you have any news?"

I filled Salinger in on everything Ethan had told me and we agreed to speak again later in the day. I hung up and went to find Ellie. From what Zak had said I felt like I might have some repair work to do on our relationship. Normally Ellie wasn't insecure, but her pregnancy hormones seemed to be doing a real number on her.

"Oh my gosh. Let me help you with that!" I said a bit too loudly when I discovered Ellie wrestling the side of the crib into a standing position.

"I'm pregnant, not an invalid," Ellie snapped when I took the side rail from her hands.

"I know that," I snapped back. Then I took a deep breath before going on. "I know you're anxious about getting the room ready for Eli, but I thought you were waiting to let Levi handle the crib."

"Levi was going to do it, but he isn't here. It seems he had errands to do that were more important than preparing for the birth of our son." Ellie sat down on the floor. A single tear escaped her eye.

I sat down across from her. "What's wrong?"

"I—don't—know," Ellie sobbed.

I leaned forward and pulled her into my arms. "How can I help? Do you want me to assemble the crib?"

Ellie wiped her face with the back of her hand. "No. Levi can do it when he gets home. I guess I'm just starting to get anxious about being ready for Eli. His official due date is past and the doctor said he could be born any day. I want him to be here, but I don't feel ready. We don't have the crib or the changing table set up and I still haven't finished painting the rocking chair I've been working on."

I held both of Ellie's hands in mine and looked her in the eye. "I know the timing of the remodel on the boathouse has been hard on you. And I know it feels like your life is in chaos and there's still so much to do to regain some semblance of order. But there are a lot of people who love you and want to help. You aren't doing this by yourself."

"I know. Like I said, I'm just being hormonal. *Will* you help me with the crib?"

I hesitated. I'd told Lani we'd pick them up in forty minutes, and based on the dozens of pieces on the floor I was pretty sure putting together the crib would take longer than that. "I do want to help with the crib. I'm going to run downstairs to get Zak's toolbox. I'll be right back."

Once I was safely out of earshot I called Lani, explained the situation, and said I might be late. Then I called Zak, who was still with the contractor, and asked him to hurry. It would take Ellie and me all day to put the crib together by ourselves, but I was sure Zak could have it assembled in no time flat.

I grabbed the toolbox and went back up the stairs to find Ellie staring thoughtfully out the window. She looked sad and a little uncertain. The uncertain was natural given the fact that she was about to have a baby, but I didn't understand the sadness.

I set the toolbox on the floor and walked up behind Ellie. I put my arms around her from behind. Her belly was so big I couldn't even reach my fingers from one hand to the other. I rested my chin on her shoulder. "Penny for your thoughts."

"I was just thinking about my mom. I wish she was here."

"Is she still in the hospital?" Rosie had planned to visit when the baby was born, but she'd fallen and broken her hip a while back. It hadn't healed correctly, so they'd had to do surgery.

"Yeah. I spoke with her earlier today and it sounds like she's going to be fine, but she's in for a long recovery." Ellie placed her hands over mine, which were still resting on her stomach. "She sounded so old. And tired. I thought her decision to sell the restaurant and move in with her friend was a good decision at the time, but now I'm not so sure. She seems sort of depressed on top of everything else."

"She's had a tough time since her fall."

"I feel like I should be there to take care of her, but most days I feel like I can hardly take care of myself."

"After Eli is here and Rosie is doing better you can arrange a visit. Maybe when you're able to see her with your own eyes you'll feel better about her situation."

"Maybe." Ellie took a step away and I dropped my hands. She looked at the crib. I could see the fatigue in her eyes. "I guess we should get started."

"Are you sure you don't want to wait for Levi?" I asked.

Ellie rubbed her belly with one hand. "Maybe we should. I am tired. Maybe I'll take a nap."

I smiled weakly at my best friend. "I think that's a good idea. And if you aren't feeling better when you wake up don't worry about dinner. I'll pick something up."

Ellie walked out of the room without answering. I knew she was concerned about her mom, but my best-friend intuition told me there was something else going on. Something she didn't want to talk about. At least not with me.

I tried to understand what she might be going through. I supposed she might be scared and unsure about what the future might hold now that she was so close to delivering. I wanted to be there for her, but I'd never been pregnant, so I could only imagine what she might be going through. Her mom was unavailable, but maybe another mom would do in a pinch. I pulled out my phone and called my own mother, who had gone through her own prebirth turmoil just three years before.

"Zoe, how nice of you to call. I was just thinking about you."

"You were?" My mom, dad, and little sister lived just down the beach and I saw them all the time.

"I wanted to take a photo on Easter to send to my family. I have an adorable purple dress for Harper and I was hoping I could talk you into wearing a purple dress as well."

I frowned. I wasn't much of a dress person and I certainly wasn't a purple dress person. "I don't have a purple dress," I eventually answered.

"I figured as much, but there's a perfect dress in your size down at the boutique. I put it on hold for you and left my credit card information as well, so all you have to do is stop by to try it on. If it fits I'll take care of the rest."

I sighed. "I don't know, Mom. I wasn't planning on wearing a dress. I'm having an Easter egg hunt for the kids and I'll need to wear something I can bend over and even get down on the ground in."

"Please, sweetheart? Just for the photo. I'm wearing a white dress with a purple sash and your father has agreed to wear a white dress shirt with a purple tie."

I groaned. I really didn't want to have to mess with trying on a dress I'd only wear for such a short time, but I finally agreed.

"Wonderful. I bought a purple tie for Zak too. Do you think he'll wear it?"

"You want Zak in the photo?"

"He's your husband and therefore part of the family," Mom reminded me.

She had a point. "Okay. I'll ask him. The reason I called has to do with something other than Easter, though. I could actually use a favor from you."

"Okay. What sort of a favor?"

"Ellie is feeling sort of down. I guess you heard Rosie had surgery and won't be able to visit as planned. I have a feeling she needs someone to talk to who's been through the whole birth thing herself. She'll be home this morning with just Alex. Do you think you could pop in and maybe see if she wants to chat? Be casual about it, though. Don't tell her I asked you to come by. She's been so moody lately,

I'm not sure how she'll respond to my asking for your help."

"I'm happy to stop by. I'll just say I wanted to scout out a background for the photo."

I smiled. "Thanks, Mom."

"And don't forget the dress. You'll need to go by today."

I groaned again. "I won't forget. I promise."

Chapter 5

By the time we arrived at Ethan's he was already in the library looking for the journal. I really hoped we'd find it hidden among the other books on the shelves; otherwise we were going to waste a lot of time. It made sense to me that Rossi would hide the journal rather than keep it on his person or in his room if he knew there were other people after it as well. But could we be sure the journal and treasure were the motive for his death, and if they were, had he been aware that someone knew about the journal and was trying to secure it for their own?

I introduced Ethan to Luke and Lani and then we each took a section of the library and began our search. Ethan had an extensive collection that seemed to be shelved by subject matter, so I was careful to return everything exactly where I'd found it. Ethan had an impressive collection. To be honest, I'm not much of a reader, preferring to get out and live life rather than stay home and read about it, but if I did ever get the bug to explore unknown topics or fictional worlds I was sure Ethan's library would be the place to find anything I might be looking for. We searched for a good forty minutes before Lani asked Ethan if he had public library books shelved with the books that belonged to him.

"No. If I take a book out of the library I leave it out on my desk so I don't forget to return it. Did you find a library book on the shelves?"

"Two of them." Lani pulled them out and held them toward him.

"That's odd." Ethan crossed the room and took the books from her. He was at eye level with the shelf, while Lani was too short to see beyond the bindings, which was why he noticed there were items stored in the space behind the books. Ethan reached his hand into the space created by removing the library books and pulled out a black leather journal and a small lockbox. The lockbox was made of metal and looked to be a foot long, six inches wide, and four inches tall. There was a gold-colored clasp on the front with a small key hole.

"That must be Charles Rossi's journal." I gasped, taking it from Ethan. The journal had a worn cover and yellowed pages. It was handwritten in a fancy script that reminded me of calligraphy, neat by impossible for me to read. I thought it must be written in a foreign language.

"Yes," Ethan agreed. "It appears to be, although as I mentioned before, Charles never actually showed it to me.

"Can anyone read this?" I asked, passing the journal back to Ethan.

"It's in Italian," Ethan informed us.

"Can you read Italian?" I wondered as I glanced at the neatly scrolled text.

"I can get by," Ethan answered. "I'm not fluent, but I think I remember enough to make sense of what's been written."

"There are translation programs you can use if you get stuck," Zak suggested.

"Yes, but somehow it seems wrong to read a hundred-year-old journal with a computer program. I'll try it on my own and see how it goes."

I looked down at the lockbox, which Ethan had set on his desk. "I don't suppose you know where the key to this box might be?"

Ethan shook his head.

"I can pick it," Zak offered. "Just give me a minute to run out to the truck and get some tools."

Luke picked up one of the library books and began to thumb through it. From the cover, it appeared to be a textbook dealing with the geology and topography of the western United States. The second book, also a textbook, which was still sitting on the table where Ethan had left it, covered the history of the Gold Rush and the mining camps that sprang up as a result.

"I wonder what he wanted with the library books," Lani mused.

"I'm not sure." I frowned as I opened the first book. There were a lot of diagrams and mathematical equations I couldn't begin to understand.

"There are a lot of caves and abandoned mines around here," Ethan pointed out. "I suppose Peter Romanov might have hidden the treasure in a cave or mineshaft. If it turns out that the location is recorded in the journal it could be Charles felt he needed to familiarize himself with the local topography to understand whatever directions Romanov left behind."

I bit my thumbnail as I considered that possibility. A cave or mineshaft would be a good place to hide a treasure as long as it was protected from the elements. It was cool and dark underground, which would help preserve the items as long as they were protected from the dampness.

Zak returned while I was pondering the likelihood that the treasure was hidden underground. He quickly picked the lock on the box and opened it. Inside was a single object: a thumb drive.

Zak picked it up and slipped it into the laptop he'd also brought in from the truck. "It's encrypted."

"Can you break it?" I asked.

Zak assured me that he could, sounding almost offended that I'd even asked. I stared at the laptop screen, which just looked like gibberish to me. Zak turned to Ethan. "I'd like to take the thumb drive to the Academy to run some scenarios though the computer."

"Fine by me. I certainly don't have the background to decrypt it myself. I'll work on the journal while you work on the thumb drive."

"I'd like to come with you," Luke said to Zak, "if that's okay."

"Sure. I could use the help." Zak glanced at me.

"I'm going to go over to the library to speak to Hazel," I responded to Zak's unasked question. "If Rossi took these books out from her maybe she helped him find what he was looking for in the first place. She might have some insight into what it was he was trying to do."

"I'll go with Zoe," Lani said. "I'm afraid computer code and Italian are beyond me."

"Okay, it sounds like we have a plan. Let's all meet back here in a few hours to compare notes," I suggested, and everyone agreed.

******

We'd all taken the same car to Ethan's, so Zak ran Lani and me back to the house to pick up my car. I could see Luke and Lani were impressed by both the size and the location of the estate Zak had bought from my grandfather several years earlier. I supposed the large property set right on the lakeshore would be impressive to those who had never seen it before, but to me it was simply home.

"Wow," Lani said when we pulled into the front drive. "This place is huge. How many square feet do you have?"

"I'm not sure. I guess maybe around twenty-five thousand. Personally, I think it's a bit much. Had I been the one to design and build the house I would have scaled back, but my grandfather, who was the one who built it, likes to do things in a grand manner. I'd like to get going to the library right now, but if you and Luke would like to come to dinner tonight I'll give you the grand tour."

Lani glanced at Luke, who said he'd enjoy a tour of the house. Lani and I climbed out of Zak's truck and headed toward my car. I unlocked it with the remote and gestured for her to get in.

"I want you to meet my best friends, Levi and Ellie, as well," I added as I got into the driver's seat. "They're living with us while my boathouse, which they live in, is being enlarged."

"I'd like to meet them. Do you and Zak have children?"

"Sort of."

Lani raised an eyebrow. "Sort of?"

"We don't have biological children, but we do have two twelve-year-olds living with us. Both have parents, so it isn't a legal arrangement, but both come from families who are unable to take care of them on a daily basis, so Zak and I stepped in." I started the car and pulled onto the drive that connected the house to the highway.

"That's really nice of you, taking on someone else's kids like that."

"Zak and I are happy to do it. We love Scooter and Alex and can't imagine life without them, although it does get tricky balancing everything once you add in Zak's responsibility to both Zimmerman Academy and Zimmerman Enterprises and mine to Zoe's Zoo, the animal shelter I own."

"It sounds like you have busy lives."

I pulled to the left and onto the highway. "We do, but I like to be busy and Zak does as well.

"I don't see how you do it." Lani settled back in her seat. "I only have me to worry about and I feel like I'm busy most of the time."

"It's funny, but before Zak and I got married and before the kids moved in with us and we started the Academy, I thought of myself as a busy person. It does seem odd that we've added so much to the mix and still have been able to keep our sanity, but I guess you adapt as you go and somehow it all works out."

"I guess." Lani didn't sound sure.

"You said you have five brothers. Do they all live in Hawaii?"

"Yes. Two of them live on Oahu, two live on Maui, and one lives on Kauai."

"You're lucky to have so many siblings. I was an only child until my sister Harper was born three years ago. I always wished for brothers and sisters."

Lani laughed. "I love my brothers, but there have been a lot of times I've wished I was an only child."

I pulled off the highway and into the parking area that served the library and other county offices. Our conversation paused while I parked and we got out of the car. Lani really was beautiful with her long, dark hair and exotic looks, and I noticed most of the men nearby had stopped what they were doing to watch her on her way into the front door of the large brick building.

"Zoe, how are you, dear?" Hazel asked as we approached her.

"I'm good." I turned to Lani. "Hazel Hampton, this is Lani Pope. She's visiting from Hawaii and is helping me out with some sleuthing today."

"I'm happy to meet you." Hazel smiled.

Lani replied in kind.

Hazel returned her attention to me. "I heard about poor Charles Rossi. Who would have wanted to hurt him?"

"That's what we're trying to find out."

"Please have a seat." Hazel motioned toward a light-colored rectangular table that was flanked by six hard plastic chairs. "How can I help?"

Lani and I sat down and I turned to Hazel. "We were at Ethan's this morning, looking for a journal he'd talked about and we came across two library books." I pulled the books out of my large bag and handed them to Hazel. "The subject matter seemed both odd and specific, so I figured they could provide a clue. I hoped you knew why he checked out these particular books."

"Mr. Rossi came in last week to ask me if I had information about Devil's Den and the mining operation in the early twentieth century. I found several journals that he looked through right at this table. He had a small black book that he referred to often. He came in several more times, asking for additional information and looking at the small black book as he did so. The last time he was in he seemed particularly interested in old records pertaining to the actual mining operation."

"What kind of records?" I asked.

"He wanted to know if there were records pertaining to the individual shafts in terms of what and how much was pulled out, and how long the mine was in operation; things like that."

"Do you have that sort of information?"

Hazel got up and walked across the room, returning with a large binder. "This is an example of the kind of reports that were left behind when the mines dried up and everyone left Devil's Den. It certainly isn't an exhaustive accounting of what was pulled out of the mines. Many of the operations were small and records for them were probably never kept. There were a few larger mines that were owned by investors, and they tended to keep better records."

I frowned. "Why would Rossi be interested in any of that?"

"Maybe he stumbled across a live vein," Lani suggested.

Hazel lowered her glasses so they were perched on the end of her nose. "Based on the information Mr. Rossi was asking for, I wouldn't be surprised to find that was true. He seemed interested in information about the mining operation that spanned a wider breadth than just the location of the shafts. Like I said, he was in several times looking through documents, and the two books you have here aren't the only ones he took out. If I had to guess, he was interested not just in the historical value of the information but in the predictive value of it as well."

"The predictive value?" I asked.

"He seemed focused on the topography in relation to the amount of gold found, as well as the identification of other minerals that had been mined. He also checked out a bunch of books on geology, so I think he was interested in the surrounding land as well."

I sat back in my chair and considered what Hazel had shared. Several things struck me as odd, but mostly I was confused as to Rossi's purpose for needing such specific information about the mines. Everyone realized there was still gold in the mines, but it had been determined long ago that the cost to extract it would far surpass its value. Unless he'd stumbled across an accessible vein no one knew about, I doubted he'd had prospecting on his mind.

"You said you saw Rossi reading a small black book. I assume it was his journal. Did you happen to get a look at it?"

"He didn't volunteer any information as to what he was doing and I didn't ask."

"You said he was in several times. Did anyone ever come in with him?"

Hazel shook her head. "No. He always came alone."

"Has anyone else checked out any books similar to these in the past week or so?" Lani asked.

I nodded. She'd asked an excellent question. If someone else was looking for the treasure and had any information about its whereabouts, they'd most likely need the same information Rossi had.

"Not that I can think of, but I can go back through my records if you think it's important."

"It could be," I answered. "If you don't mind."

"Of course I don't mind," Hazel said before heading into her office.

"Do you think Rossi found a vein of gold while looking for what Peter Romanov left and got sidetracked?" Lani asked.

I paused to consider the question. "I don't think that's it. Charles Rossi was an educated man who would probably realize the cost to recover any gold left behind most likely exceeded its value. There had to be another reason he was interested in records pertaining to specific mines. I suppose the yield of a specific mine could be part of the clue. Perhaps we'd have a better idea as to what he was after once Ethan translates the journal and Zak decrypts the thumb drive."

I glanced up as Hazel returned to the room. "Did you find anything?"

"No one other than Charles has checked out books similar to the ones he was looking at for quite some time."

"Can you think of anything else Rossi did or said that might help us understand exactly what he was thinking?"

Hazel paused and tapped her chin with an index finger. "He asked me for three phone numbers and addresses. All three were listed, so I didn't think there was any harm in giving him something he could have found himself in the phone directory."

"Whose number did he want?" I asked.

"One was for a store that sells old camping and prospecting equipment, a hardware store, and a store that sold handguns. I gave him the phone numbers for Outback Hunting and Fishing, Ace Hardware, and Doug's Guns and Ammo."

I bit my lip and narrowed my eyes. "I wonder if Rossi knew he was in danger. It would explain his desire to buy a gun."

"If someone was following him or watching him, he might have known what was going on," Lani answered. "I'm also wondering if the boat he was pushed from was owned by someone locally or if it was a rental. It might be worth our while to visit the local marinas and ask around."

"Good idea." I glanced at Hazel. "Rossi was seen dining with a man at least six feet four inches tall with gray-streaked hair. Does that ring a bell with you?"

"Owen Gallo."

"Who's Owen Gallo?" I asked.

"Owen is the new owner at Outback Hunting and Fishing. He's a tall, fit man with gray-streaked hair. Not a lot of men in Ashton Falls are that tall, other than Zak, of course."

"I don't think I've ever met him."

"He's only been in town a month, or maybe two. I happened to meet him while I was having lunch with Gilda." Gilda Reynolds owned Bears and Beavers, a shop that sold touristy items featuring bears and beavers. Her shop shared an alley with Outback Hunting and Fishing, so it made sense the two would be acquainted.

After a minute I said, "Maybe Rossi went to Outback Hunting and Fishing to buy camping and perhaps even prospecting supplies. While he was there he might have struck up a conversation with Gallo. Maybe Rossi realized Gallo could help him in some way and cut him into a deal. Of course if Gallo was new to Ashton Falls he wouldn't be any more knowledgeable about the area than Rossi, but maybe he possessed a specific skill of some sort."

"If he owns a hunting and fishing supply store he most likely either owns or has access to a boat," Lani added.

"And guns. Outback didn't sell handguns in the past, but they've always sold hunting rifles. It couldn't hurt to stop by to chat with Gallo. In fact, it would probably be a good idea to stop by in all three locations Rossi inquired about."

"You should check with your dad too," Hazel suggested. "I didn't specifically give him the phone number and address for Donovan's because he didn't ask for it, but your dad sells the sort of items one might need if one planned on going camping, especially at this time of year."

"I will," I answered. "We'll go there after we chat with Gallo. And thanks for the leads. Hopefully, Gallo will have some insight into what was on Rossi's mind."

"If he isn't the killer, that is," Lani murmured.

"Yeah, there's always that."

Chapter 6

Lani and I headed back toward my car. We had just buckled ourselves in when my phone beeped. I groaned. It was my mother, reminding me to try on the dress she'd picked out.

"Something wrong?" Lani asked.

"Not really wrong. More like inconvenient. The text was from my mother. She wants me to stop by the boutique to try on a dress she's picked out for me to wear for Easter."

Lani raised a brow. "Does your mother often pick out your clothes?"

I put the key into the ignition and started the car before answering. "No. She wants us to take a family photo and everyone has to have on purple and white. I'm not a dress person and would much rather wear slacks or even shorts, weather permitting, but Mom has been on a photography kick ever since Harper was born and tries to take photos for every important occasion."

Lani smiled as I pulled onto the highway. "That's nice. You said your sister is three?"

I nodded.

"I know this is none of my business, and you don't have to answer, but why did she wait so long to have a second child? There has to be at least a twenty-five-year age difference between the two of you."

I turned onto the side road where boutique was located. "My mom and dad divorced when I was very young and my dad raised me. They reunited briefly almost four years ago and Harper was conceived. Mom left Ashton Falls before she knew she was pregnant, but once she realized she was she returned to Ashton Falls and, after a rocky courtship, they remarried." I pulled into the boutique parking lot. "I'm happy to say they're blissfully happy this time around, and while I'm not fond of my mom's occasional desire to dress me, I'm happy, too, that we're finally a family."

"What a nice story. I'm happy things worked out for all of you."

I parked the car and turned off the engine. I sat for a moment looking at the frilly dresses displayed in the window. I only hoped Mom hadn't picked out something with a lot of lace and a big skirt. Lani and I headed to the front door.

"Zoe," the proprietor greeted me. "I'm so glad you made it in. I have the dress set aside for you."

I turned to Lani. "Why don't you go ahead and look around? I'll only be a minute."

I followed the woman down the hall to the dressing room. She handed me a purple dress that didn't seem too bad. It was summery, with short sleeves and a hem that looked as if it would hit me midshin. I quickly peeled off my jeans and shirt and slipped the dress over my head. I glanced in the mirror and quickly decided it was something I could stand to wear for an hour while Mom got the photos she wanted. I took off the dress, pulled my street clothes back on, and took it to the front of the store, where Lani was chatting with the owner.

"So, how'd we do?" the woman asked.

"We did fine. Did Mom already pay for it or do you need a credit card?"

"Your mom left instructions for me to charge it to her account. I'm happy the dress worked out for you. Your mom spent hours trying to pick out the perfect dresses for her girls."

Despite the fact that I really wasn't into purple dresses, it warmed my heart that my mom had taken the time to pick out dresses for Harper and me. I remembered all the years I'd missed her, longing for her to show an interest in me. Purple might not be my favorite color, but I supposed it was the thought that counted, so I waited while the woman carefully wrapped the dress, then took it and headed out to the car.

"It's really a pretty shade of purple," Lani offered.

"Yeah, it wasn't as bad as I thought it might be, and I guess it'll be nice to have a family portrait. Let's head over to Outback Hunting and Fishing, and then we'll check in with the guys to see where they are with the encryption thing."

"It's nice of Zak to let Luke help out. I imagine he doesn't really need anyone's help."

"Zak is really, really smart. He has stuff in his head, especially in relation to mathematics and computers, that most people, myself included, can't even begin to comprehend. But he's also a really good guy who never flaunts his genius and always goes out of his way to include people in his projects." I turned left to head back toward Main Street, where

Outback Hunting and Fishing was located. "There was this one time when one of his biggest customers got hacked. Zak spent days trying to chase down the hacker, who somehow managed to stay one step ahead of him. When Zak finally isolated him and found out who he was, it turned out it was a sixteen-year-old high-school dropout."

Lani looked as surprised as I'd felt when I'd first heard it myself. "What did he do?"

"He brought Pi home and gave him a job and an education. He's in college right now, and Zak plans to make him a partner in his company after he graduates."

Lani shook her head. "Most people would have just had the kid arrested."

"Zak said that if the kid could stay one step ahead of him for almost a week he deserved the best education money could buy. Pi has a real talent and will be a huge asset to Zak in the long run, so it turned out to be a win-win thing." I pulled into the parking lot. "We're here. I just hope this Owen Gallo is in a talkative mood."

Outback Hunting and Fishing was what I thought of as a man's store, although women could be in to hunting and fishing as well. Personally, I don't have the stomach for either. Still, I've always enjoyed the woodsy feel of the store, stuffed wildlife notwithstanding. While I don't appreciate the heads of elk, deer, moose, and even bear on the walls, I do enjoy the real log walls, the dark green carpet, and the floor-to-ceiling river-rock fireplace.

"Can I help you?" asked a man so tall it had Lani and me both straining our necks to look up to his face. He had a deep voice and a strong Italian accent that caused his words to roll off his tongue in a rather fascinating fashion.

"My name is Zoe," I introduced myself to the man, who looked to be in his early sixties and was not only tall but broad-shouldered and attractive. I had a feeling that in addition to buying the store he lived the outdoor lifestyle. "I live in town. And this is my friend, Lani. We wanted to ask you about a friend we have in common."

The man raised one bushy gray brow. "What friend?"

"Charles Rossi."

The man narrowed his gaze. "You are a friend of Charles?"

"I am," I said, exaggerating a bit. I mean, I'd been introduced to him and had spoken to him once. I wasn't certain that classified us as friends, but I decided to go with it. "I spoke to him a couple of days ago and he told me that he planned to come in here to talk to you about camping equipment."

The man looked amused. "He told you that, did he?"

"He did." I tried for a confidence I didn't feel.

"Then perhaps you misunderstood. Charles did not speak to me about any camping equipment."

Okay, now what? I guess I should have come in with a plan; I had no idea how to segue into a discussion about whether this man had killed Charles Rossi or knew who did.

"I guess you heard Charles was found dead," Lani stepped in, I imagine as a response to the look of panic on my face.

"I had heard." The man momentarily lowered his eyes before continuing in a deep baritone voice. "What does his accident have to do with the equipment you say he was interested in purchasing?"

Lani wandered around the store, picking something up, looking at it, then setting it back down before looking the man in the eye. "We believe Charles didn't die as the result of an accident. We believe he was murdered. We also believe the reason he was murdered may have something to do with his activities during the past couple of days, which include a visit with you, where he may have discussed camping equipment."

He frowned. "It seems to me that you little girls should look elsewhere for your answers. I know nothing about any interest in camping equipment or a visit to my store. I am a busy man and must get back to work."

Little girls? His comment didn't sit well with me and I was willing to bet it didn't sit well with Lani either. I was about to say something to defend our right to look anywhere we chose for our answers when Lani walked over to the climbing wall set up in the back of the store. "May I?"

"You have experience climbing the wall?" he asked, doubt evident on his face. The wall was at least twenty feet high.

"I can't say I've actually climbed a wall like this, but it doesn't look very hard."

He chuckled. "It is harder than it looks and not for little girls."

Lani looked him directly in the eye. "If I can climb this wall in less than sixty seconds will you agree to answer any questions my friend might have?"

He narrowed his gaze. He looked Lani up and down and I could tell he found her lacking. She was, after all, only about five feet tall and couldn't weigh more than a hundred pounds soaking wet. "You have a deal. If you can climb the wall to the top in less than sixty seconds I will answer your questions, but if you can't you will go away and leave me alone."

Lani looked at me. I nodded. She might be petite, but I'd seen what a strong swimmer she was and was willing to bet she was a strong climber as well. Lani agreed to the man's terms and then scrambled up the wall like a mountain goat, taking less than sixty seconds to do so. The man looked amazed as he watched her accomplish the feat without even breaking a sweat.

"How'd I do?" Lani asked as she looked down from the top of the wall, where she hung by one hand that was clutched to a grip. She looked so relaxed and comfortable, she gave the impression she could stay there all day.

"That is amazing, but I think you lied about not climbing before."

Lani grabbed a nearby rope and rappelled down to the floor. She landed smoothly like a cat, then smiled at the man with white teeth that shone from her bronze skin. "I didn't say I'd never climbed before; I said I'd never climbed a wall like this."

"How very clever of you. It seems you have tricked me, but a deal is a deal. What do you want to know?"

Lani glanced in my direction, turning the conversation over to me.

I asked my first question. "As Lani has already informed you, we don't believe Charles's death was an accident. We believe he was murdered. That may have something to do with camping equipment he bought or intended to buy, but as far as I know you were the last person who saw him alive, so you might have some idea what it was that got him killed."

"You think I killed him?"

I crossed my arms over my chest. "Did you?"

"Of course not."

"Then if you didn't kill him why don't you help us figure out who did?"

He raised a brow. "And how am I supposed to do that?"

I walked across the store and leaned against a counter. "You can start by telling me what sort of equipment Charles bought from you, and then you can tell me what you and Charles were chatting about during dinner on Wednesday night. And don't leave anything out. I want all the details, capiche?"

I was amazed when he laughed. "You're a cheeky one, I'll give you that. If you must know, Charles and I met when he came in to buy climbing equipment, not camping equipment."

"Climbing equipment?" I asked. It had seemed to me that Rossi was old and not in very good shape. I couldn't imagine he'd had the strength to climb the wall in the store, let alone a mountain, so why in the world would he be buying climbing equipment?

Owen Gallo looked at me. "Charles was not as agile as your friend here, but he did seem to understand the fundamentals of climbing, and he said he was in this area to do some exploration. In addition to climbing equipment he purchased a miner's hat with a light on it, a compass, and a few other items one might need if they were going spelunking. I asked him if he planned to explore the old mines and he told me exploring them were on his bucket list. I warned him of the dangers of such a thing and he said he would take precautions. I've done quite a bit of cave exploration, so we chatted for a while and I gave him some tips."

He took a deep breath before he continued. "A couple of days later he came in again and invited me to dinner. He wanted to ask my opinion about the likelihood of his finding a specific type of mineral in this area. I explained that I was new to Ashton Falls and not the best person to ask, but he said he was tired of eating alone and would enjoy my company anyway. I had nothing else to do that night and was going to get a free meal out of it, so I agreed to meet him at the restaurant."

"Did he tell you what sort of mineral he was looking for?" I asked.

"Azurite."

"And what is azurite?"

"It's a soft, deep blue copper."

"Do you know why he was interested in this particular mineral?"

"He didn't say. It is quite beautiful and is often used to make jewelry. There are also people who believe it has healing powers."

"Did he ask you any other questions?" I continued.

He shook his head.

"Did the two of you part ways when you left the restaurant that night?" I asked.

I watched his face closely as he replied. "Yes. We said good-bye and I never saw him again."

I paused to try to sort out my thoughts. What did Rossi want with azurite? I doubted he wanted to make jewelry. Maybe the mineral was a clue. Maybe Peter Romanov had told Antonio Rossi that the treasure was hidden in a cave with blue rocks.

"You told him you didn't know where to find azurite in Ashton Falls. Did you refer him to someone else who might?" I asked.

"Yes, I did. I suggested he speak to Mac Walters. He is an old prospector who knows the area a lot better than I ever will."

Made sense. If there was azurite around here Mac would know where to find it. The problem was finding Mac. He was something of a hermit who moved around, living off the land. I asked Gallo if he knew where he was these days, and he said he didn't know for sure but had recommended that Rossi try one of the local bars because Mac liked to drink. He wished us luck and conveyed his condolences for Charles's passing.

"What do you think?" Lani asked after we left the store.

"I think you're a monkey. How did you learn to climb like that?"

"I work out all the time. I've been waiting for my number to come up with an invitation to the police academy, and when that happens I want to be ready, mentally *and* physically. I know my brothers think I'll never pass the physical part of the entrance requirements, but I can assure you I will. I may be tiny, but there's a lot of power and agility behind my ninety-eight pounds. I'll not only pass the agility test; I plan to own it."

I put my hand up in a high five. "You go girl. If you make the cut and take the test I'd love to be there to see you wipe up the floor with the doubters."

Lani grinned. Once again I felt the certainty that we were kindred spirits.

"Do you know where to find this Mac Walters?" Lani asked.

"Mac is well known in Ashton Falls. He basically lives nowhere and everywhere. He moves around a lot and mostly lives off the land, although he isn't above taking a handout when offered one. Gallo was right; Mac does love his whiskey, so I'll probably start by visiting some of the local bars. If he's around someone will have seen him, although it's early for him to have arrived on the mountain."

"He's lives somewhere else in the winter?"

"Yeah. He goes down the mountain then, where there's less snow and the temps are warmer. He usually doesn't come back up here until late May or early June, but we've had a really mild spring so he may have come early this year."

"So what now?" Lani asked.

"Let's head back to Ethan's. I'm interested in finding out what the journal says. Maybe it mentions blue rock as a clue. Hopefully Zak and Luke will be there and we can regroup." I glanced at my watch. "We still have a few hours before we need to be back for dinner, but I don't want to be late. Ellie is making her famous lasagna."

"That's nice of her."

"Ellie is my very best friend and the best cook I know. She's a sweet, giving person I think you'll really like her, but be forewarned: She's *very* pregnant and hormones are really doing a number on her. If she begins to cry for no reason, or gets mad and stomps off in a huff, don't take it personally. The poor thing is a bundle of emotions waiting to explode."

"Okay, I'm forewarned. When my sister-in-law was pregnant she was such a mess I pretty much swore never, ever to put myself through such a barbaric method of procreation."

I laughed. "You don't want kids?"

"No, I don't," Lani said with conviction.

"And Luke?"

Lani shrugged. "I don't know. He has genuine affection for the horses he raises and seems to get along with people of all ages, even kids. He's caring, patient, and understanding, and I'm sure he'd be a good dad. Both of his sisters are about to have babies and I've noticed a look of longing in his eyes a time or two when we've spoken of them. The thing is, I'm not sure it's because he wants children of his own or if he just misses his family. We've never really talked about it. How about you? Do you and Zak plan to have children?"

"Eventually."

I didn't elaborate and I didn't blame Lani for not wanting children. I hadn't either until very recently. It was actually Alex who'd opened my heart to the possibility and Zak who'd shown me what a committed relationship could be. I surreptitiously touched my hand to my stomach. Zak and I had decided to try for a baby a while back. It hadn't happened and we'd decided to take a break from trying. But, looking into the future, I knew we were meant to have children of our own, so maybe it was time to get back on the horse—metaphorically, of course—and give it another try.

Chapter 7

Zak and Luke were already back at Ethan's by the time we returned. Ethan had found and begun to translate the passage in the journal that seemed to deal with Peter Romanov's treasure. I asked him if he'd noticed a mention of azurite and he said that, coincidentally, there was something about the treasure being buried with blue stone. I filled the others in on the fact that Rossi had purchased climbing equipment and taken the new owner of Outback Hunting and Fishing to dinner to ask about local deposits of azurite.

Ethan hadn't had a chance to translate the entire section regarding the treasure, but based on what he'd read so far it could very well be that Romanov had hidden the treasure in a cave or mineshaft, although he hadn't found anything that said that specifically.

"The thing that's bothering me," I said, "is that a hundred years ago when Romanov would have hidden the treasure, the mines were being worked. It doesn't seem likely that hiding something where there were not only men working but dynamiting going on as well, would have been a good choice."

"Maybe the mine he chose was dry," Lani suggested. "Or it was a cave and not a mine where he hid the treasure."

"Did you manage to decrypt the thumb drive?" I asked Zak.

"Not yet, but I will. Whoever did the encryption wasn't an amateur; this was done with a sophisticated program. In fact, it's something I've never seen before. That doesn't mean I can't crack it; it just means it will take more time. I left a program running on the big computer at the Academy. I'm hoping it will provide me with the information I need to figure out the best way in. I was planning to go back to check on it after we finish here."

"Is the drive safe?" Ethan looked concerned.

"If you're worried someone can get into the computer room at the Academy and steal it, the answer is no. The security I have on that place is better than the government uses to protect Fort Knox."

Ethan looked relieved.

"I have an idea about the azurite," Zak added as he pulled out his laptop and began typing at the speed of light. After several minutes he stopped and jotted something down on a piece of paper. "According to the mining records that have been digitized, which I'll admit are limited in comparison to the entire mining operation in Devil's Den, it looks like we can find azurite at this location."

I looked down at the paper. It looked like Zak had written down coordinates for longitude and latitude.

"Is that close by?" I asked.

"The deposit should be in Shadow Mountain, which is about thirty miles from here."

"Question," Lani piped up. "While I love a treasure hunt as much as the next person, do we believe that finding the treasure, if it's even still there, will help us reveal the identity of the person who killed Charles Rossi?"

No one responded, probably because no one had an answer. It seemed the treasure and Rossi's death were related, and if they were, solving one mystery might give us clues about the other, but it was possible Rossi's death and the treasure weren't connected at all.

"I guess all we can do is follow the leads we uncover to see where they take us," I eventually said.

"What about the other places the librarian mentioned?" Lani asked. "Ace Hardware, Doug's Guns and Ammo, and your father's store. Should we follow up with those as well?"

I nodded. "We should, although if we don't go soon, we won't be able to make it out to Shadow Mountain and back before we need to be home for dinner. Let's head out and I'll call the other people on Hazel's list on the way. If I get the sense we should follow up in more depth with anyone we can do that tomorrow."

The drive to Shadow Mountain took about thirty minutes in each direction, which meant we'd have less than an hour there if we were to get home for dinner at the time Ellie and I had decided upon. No matter what we found I wasn't going to risk tears or anger by being even a minute late. As her best friend, I needed to do everything in my power to make things easier for Ellie.

Luke and Lani rode with Ethan in his car while I went with Zak in his truck. I decided to make the phone calls to my dad at Donovan's, Doug's Guns and Ammo, and Ace Hardware first thing in case I lost cell service when we made our way out of town. My dad was with a customer when I called and couldn't talk long, but he said Rossi had come in at the beginning of the week to purchase several flashlights, a bunch of batteries, a shovel, and bolt cutters. The man I spoke to at Ace Hardware informed me that he didn't remember anyone fitting Rossi's description, but anything Rossi might have bought from the hardware store he could have just as easily purchased from Donovan's.

Doug, from Doug's Guns and Ammo, told me a man fitting Rossi's description had been in looking at guns but hadn't bought anything. Doug said the man seemed nervous, and he was sure he'd never shot a gun before, so he'd done his best to sway him away from purchasing one until he'd visited a shooting range and maybe taken a safety class.

Based on the items Rossi bought from Outback Hunting and Fishing, combined with the ones he purchased from Donovan's, it seemed clear to me that he had spelunking on his mind. But I still had several unanswered questions. The first had to do with the likelihood that Peter Romanov, who had stopped at Devil's Den on his way east due to illness, would have had the strength to hide the treasure in a location that appeared to require climbing supplies to access. The whole thing made no sense. The longer I thought about it, the more certain I was that there was more to this mystery than met the eye.

The elevation at the foot of Shadow Mountain was quite a bit higher than Ashton Falls; once we got to the dirt road leading from the highway to the old mining camp and began our climb, snow began to appear on the side of the road. Not only was the ground still covered with it but the temperature dropped significantly, making me wish I'd brought a heavier jacket.

"It definitely looks like someone has been up here since the last snow," Zak commented as he nodded to several sets of tire tracks evident in the snow on both sides of the road.

Zak pulled over and consulted his compass. Then he turned onto a side road that was in a lot worse shape than even the dirt road we'd taken in. He drove slowly because it was overgrown with foliage and deeply rutted. After a few minutes he pulled over to the side and turned off the engine. "I think we'll need to walk from here, if we actually want to look for azurite, though I'm beginning to think this isn't the lead we're after. According to what Rossi told Ethan, Peter Romanov was ill and died in the clinic in

Devil's Den. The distance from there to here is at least thirty miles; combined with the rise in altitude it would be quite a trek on horseback, especially if you were ill." Zak looked down at the compass. It appeared he was doing some quick calculations in his head. "It looks like the longitude and latitude coordinates we have would put us just about in the center of that mountain." He pointed in the distance.

"We have to climb the mountain?"

"No, I don't think so. I'm guessing there's a mine entrance that will take us in from the side."

I looked behind us to where Ethan had pulled his car over. Lani climbed out and began jumping around in the snow. I couldn't help but smile. I opened my door and got out.

"I take it you like snow?" I asked.

"Oh my. It's awesome. I've only ever seen it one other time in my life and that was when I was a child. I'd hoped you would still have some here when Luke suggested we borrow his uncle's cabin and was disappointed when we arrived and found that it had already melted."

I grinned. "I'm glad we could provide you with the snow experience."

"So is this the location?" Lani asked.

I glanced over to where Zak was speaking with Ethan and Luke. "No. According to Zak, the spot we're looking for is in the middle of that mountain."

Lani frowned as she looked in the direction I was pointing. "We're going to climb that mountain?"

"No. Zak thinks there must be a mine entrance that will take us into the mountain. We don't really have time to check it out today. Zak doesn't think Romanov would have hidden the treasure this far from Devil's Den and I have to agree." I looked around. "Although a mine like this would explain the equipment Rossi bought, which makes me wonder where that equipment is. Salinger didn't say anything about finding climbing gear in his motel room."

"Perhaps it was in his car," Lani suggested.

Now that I thought of it, Salinger hadn't said anything about Rossi's car either. I'd have to call him when we got close enough to town to pick up cell service.

Lani and I joined the men to ask what they were planning. Now that the novelty of snow had worn off I could see that Lani, whose sweatshirt was thinner than mine, was shivering. The wind blew steadily this high up in the mountains, making for a chilly experience if one wasn't dressed properly.

"What are you thinking?" I asked them.

Zak looked up at the mountain. "Maybe we should see what's on the thumb drive and then decide what to do next. As I said, the encryption is tricky, but I'm sure I can get in by tomorrow at the latest."

Ethan nodded. "I think that might be the best plan. For one thing, it's freezing up here. If we do decide to come back we'll need to make sure we have warmer clothing and plenty of flashlights and emergency supplies. Let's touch base tomorrow."

Luke and Lani rode back with Zak and me; we'd drop them off at their cabin so they could clean up and pick up their own rental car before heading home to check on Ellie and the dinner she was preparing.

Chapter 8

Zak dropped me off at the house and then headed back to Zimmerman Academy to check on the progress of the decryption program he'd left running. He said he'd probably bring the thumb drive home with him so he could continue to work on it later this evening, but he hoped the much more powerful hard drives the school owned would have made a significant amount of progress in narrowing things down while he was away.

I headed in through the side door, which led directly into the mudroom located off the kitchen. I was greeted there by Charlie, who launched immediately into the happy dog dance, and the smell of something wonderful cooking in the oven. I slipped off my shoes, which were muddy from our trek up the mountain, picked Charlie up and cuddled him against my chest, and continued into the kitchen, were Ellie and

Alex were chatting while chopping veggies at the counter.

"What smells so good?" I asked as I walked in and got a full blast of the smell of something Italian coming from the oven.

"Lasagna," Ellie answered. "I made sausage and seafood."

"I love seafood lasagna. Did you include lobster with the crab and shrimp?"

"Of course. And scallops too."

My stomach began grumbling loudly, so I went over to the counter to snag one of the carrots Alex had been chopping for the salad. I was ravenous and couldn't wait for dinner to be served. "It smells and sounds wonderful. I'm starving and I'm sure the others will be as well." I frowned. "I guess we forgot to eat lunch."

"Dinner will be another hour, but I have homemade bread cooling on the rack. There's plenty if you want to grab a piece to tide you over," Ellie suggested.

I set Charlie on the floor, then padded across the room in my stocking feet. "I thought you weren't going to overdo," I said as I broke a large piece of bread from the loaf. "Making homemade bread seems like overdoing to me."

"I didn't overdo," Ellie argued. "I was feeling better today and Alex helped a lot.

We even managed to get Baby Eli's room finished, which means he can make his appearance at any time and we'll be ready."

I smiled at Alex. I knew how much it meant to Ellie to be ready for the baby before his arrival. I'd felt sort of bad for not staying to help, but I really did want to find out who killed Charles Rossi and if and how it related to the treasure.

"I'm going to run upstairs, take a quick shower, and change, but then I'll be back to help," I told the pair.

"Zak isn't with you?" Ellie looked toward the door.

"He went back to check on a program he's running on the computer at the Academy, but he'll be here in plenty of time for dinner."

"And your friends?"

I paused and glanced at Ellie. "They should be here in about an hour. Are Levi and Scooter around?"

"In the game room, battling the forces of evil."

It occurred to me that Scooter was probably thrilled to have another person in the household to play games with when Zak wasn't around.

I left the kitchen, headed down the hall, and poked my head in the game room. I stood in the entry and greeted Levi and Scooter. Neither answered; by the look of things, they were so involved in their game that neither even realized I was in the room. I headed back down the hall and up the stairs. As soon as I entered the bedroom, I closed the door, then peeled off the clothes I had worn all day. I padded across the room to the attached bath and turned on the shower. I let the water warm for a minute, then stepped into the steaming hot shower and let the water run over my head and down my back. It had been cold up on that mountain and I felt like my insides still hadn't warmed up. After a few minutes I squeezed some rain-scented shampoo into my palm and began rubbing it into my hair.

As I washed my hair I thought about the evening ahead. For some inexplicable reason, it was really important to me that Levi and Ellie and Luke and Lani all love each other as much as I loved them. Okay, I supposed *love* was a strong word, but I really wanted them to get along. Luke and Lani would be returning home in ten days, but I didn't think it would be outside the realm of possibility that Zak and I could visit Hawaii, and maybe we could bring Levi and Ellie along after Baby Eli was born.

I rinsed my hair and then applied a thick conditioner in a matching scent. Levi and Ellie and Zak and I had taken trips together in the past, and I couldn't help wondering what having a baby would do to the couple time we were used to sharing. Sure, now they were basically living with us, so we'd see them all the time, but what about after Eli was born? Would they still have time not only to vacation with us but to sleuth with us as well? I had purposely tried not to draw them into this specific investigation due to Ellie's condition, but I was certain that as long as there were bad guys I'd be out catching them, and I had to wonder how the sleuthing dynamic would be altered with a baby added to the mix.

After I rinsed the conditioner from my hair, I turned the water off and stepped out of the shower. I wrapped my hair in a large cream-colored towel and then my body in another. I opened the bathroom door to let the steam escape and went barefoot into the bedroom to find something to wear for our informal dinner party. Deciding on a pair of black leggings topped with a light blue sweater, I dressed and then went back into the bathroom to do something with my hair.

I looked at my reflection in the mirror, combed a brush through my hair, and allowed my thoughts to drift to the murder case/treasure hunt we'd worked on that day. Normally by this point I had a list of suspects to interview and then methodically eliminate. I had to ask myself if there was even one suspect to put on a list I'd yet to establish. Initially, the fact that Owen Gallo had dined with Charles Rossi on the evening before he was found dead would be as good a clue as any, but while the guy was a bit of a chauvinist, I hadn't picked up the psycho killer vibe when we'd spoken to him that afternoon. I remembered that Rossi had been in some sort of an altercation with a man wearing a dark hoodie at around nine o'clock that night, which meant that whatever had happened to him, had occurred after that.

I still needed to call Salinger to ask him about the climbing equipment and Rossi's car, and to see if he had any news, so I grabbed my cell and sat down on the corner of the bed.

"I was wondering when I'd hear from you," Salinger said.

"I was out of service this afternoon so it had to wait. Before I get sidetracked, I want to ask about some climbing equipment Rossi bought. Did you find it in his room when you searched it?"

"Nope," Salinger answered gruffly. "Didn't see anything like that."

"How about his car? It occurred to me that the equipment could be in his trunk. I don't suppose you searched the trunk?"

"Didn't search the trunk because we don't have the car."

Okay, that seemed like it might be a clue. If the car wasn't found at the motel Rossi must have driven to wherever it was he met up with his killer rather than the killer nabbing him from his room. "Have you looked for the car in the obvious places?" I asked.

"If by obvious places you mean the local marinas, yeah. So far the car hasn't turned up anywhere I've looked. I did get the license number from the motel clerk, so I have an APB out for it."

I was surprised the clerk had bothered to record the license plate number. From what Salinger had already told me about him, he hadn't seemed to be too on the ball.

"I have a lead I haven't been able to verify yet," Salinger began.

"Really? What lead?"

He cleared his throat before he continued. "I stopped by Rosie's to grab some lunch and the new waitress told me that Rossi had been in there for lunch on Monday." Salinger was referring to the restaurant Ellie's mother had owned several years back.

"Which new waitress?"

"I forget her name, but she has short brown hair and long, long legs."

I knew exactly who he meant, but I couldn't think of her name either. "Was he with anyone?"

"He was, but she's new here and didn't know the guy's name. Based on her description, I think it might have been Will."

"Our Will?" Will Danner was a teacher at Zimmerman Academy who specialized in mathematics and computer science. He was off all week for spring break, the same as everyone else. I thought of the encrypted thumb drive. Will would most likely have the ability to come up with something like that; I wondered if he hadn't helped Rossi with that part of what he'd been doing during the final days of his life.

"Yep. I tried to call him, but he didn't answer his phone. I went by his place, but he wasn't home. I know he's off work this week, but if you see him will you let him know I've been trying to contact him?"

"I will. And I'll mention it to Zak when he gets home."

"I appreciate it. Having lunch with a man doesn't necessarily mean you would know what he was up to, but the leads are so few, I'm following up on everything, even the baby buggy situation."

"What baby buggy situation?"

"Apparently, Rossi was seen sorting through a woman's baby buggy, which she'd stepped away from in the craft shop in town."

"Was there a baby in the buggy?" I asked.

"No. The woman was holding the baby. I guess she didn't want to hold the baby *and* push the buggy, so she'd left it in a corner. When she went back to it she found Rossi leaning over it and doing something with the blankets. She confronted him and he apologized, saying he was confused and thought the buggy was his daughter's."

I couldn't imagine what Rossi would have wanted with the blankets in a baby buggy. It made no sense to me. Maybe the guy had been losing his mind and everything we'd found so far was simply sending us on a wild-goose chase. I said as much to Salinger, and he agreed that nothing really made sense. He added that the woman with the baby had noticed Rossi in the consignment shop she'd visited just before the craft store. She wondered if maybe he was following her.

I shifted my position. "Why would he do that?"

"I have no idea. This case is getting stranger and stranger and I'd like to get it wrapped up sooner rather than later."

I hung up with Salinger and quickly dried my hair, slipped on some shoes, and headed downstairs. I could hear Levi speaking to Zak in the kitchen, so I went in that direction. They were talking baseball, which didn't interest me at the moment, so I interrupted to ask about the thumb drive.

"The program I ran managed to isolate the type of code that was used. I brought it home to work on after dinner. I should be able to get into it before the end of the evening if my suspicion about it is correct."

"Don't you think it's weird that Rossi, who Ethan introduced as a history professor, would have the skill to encrypt something that's taken you hours to crack? Well, I just spoke to Salinger, who said a waitress at Rosie's saw Rossi having lunch with someone who looked like Will. It occurred to me that Rossi might have enlisted Will's help with the encryption."

"Did Salinger ask Will about it?"

"He called him and even stopped by his house, but he wasn't home and hasn't returned his call. Salinger asked us to let Will know he wants to talk to him if we see him."

Zak frowned. "I hope Will is okay."

"You think he might not be?"

Zak narrowed his eyes and bit his lip. I could see he was considering what to say. "I have no reason to believe Will isn't fine, though this encryption is exactly the kind of thing he'd come up with. It's both difficult and elegant, something I've learned to expect from a lot of work Will does. I'm not trying to raise any red flags, but it bothers me that he had lunch with a man who turned up dead shortly after."

"Maybe we can take a run over to his place later," I suggested. "He may just have had a dead battery on his phone."

"That's a good idea. I think I'll call him now as well. He may have a reason to avoid Salinger but pick up a call from me."

Zak went upstairs to make his call and change for dinner. Will was such a great guy; I really hoped he hadn't gotten involved in whatever had gotten Charles Rossi killed.

Chapter 9

Will didn't answer Zak's call either, so he left a message. The fact that he wasn't answering his phone wasn't necessarily a cause for alarm. He was, after all, on vacation from the Academy. He could simply have gone somewhere for spring break that didn't have cell service: a cruise or a camping trip or something. It also wasn't necessarily odd that he hadn't informed us of his plans. He was single and unencumbered, which meant he was only responsible to himself.

Not long after Zak emerged from the bedroom, showered, and dressed in slacks and a sweater, Luke and Lani arrived. After introducing them to Ellie, Levi, Alex, and Scooter, we gave the couple a tour of the house while Alex and Levi helped Ellie get dinner on the table. I wasn't sure why exactly, but I found I was nervous about the evening, hoping it would be relaxing and enjoyable for everyone.

"This house is really spectacular," Lani murmured as I led them out onto the patio, where the indoor/outdoor pool and spa were located. "The view of the lake must be amazing during the day."

"It is a pretty great view," I agreed. Luke and Zak went to look at the gaming room while Lani and I continued to chat. "I especially love sitting out here in the summer with the roof rolled back. Although living on the ocean, as you do, must make for spectacular views too. I've always thought it would be amazing to live right on the beach, with waves crashing on to the shore."

"I have a great spot, but as far as views go it's pretty much limited to the small strip of beach and water where the condominium building is located," Lani answered. "Still, I enjoy the fact that there's a beach to run on, and I love listening to the sound of the waves at night. If you want to talk views, though, you have to come to Oahu sometime and visit us at Luke's ranch. Not only are there acres and acres of green pasture but his home is built up on a bluff with a panoramic view of the entire coastline."

"Wow. That does sound great. I'd love to come to Oahu and experience the island through your eyes. It seems like you really love your island home."

Lani nodded. "It's the heart of my family. There are a lot of things in life I'm uncertain of, but I know for a fact that I'll never leave."

"I guess I used to feel that way about Ashton Falls, but now I know my heart belongs not to a place but a person."

Lani looked confused at first, but then her eyes grew large as a light bulb went on. "You're speaking of Zak."

I nodded. "I love Ashton Falls and will be perfectly happy to live out my life here, but one day, if it becomes necessary for Zak to change location for some reason, I know I'll be just as happy living wherever his life takes him."

"What about your life? Doesn't it count?"

I nodded. "It does, and I've made my choice."

Lani didn't answer, and so I suggested showing her the home theater and gaming room, while Zak led Luke to the climate-controlled computer room and library. By the time we'd finished showing the couple around the entire house, Ellie was calling out that dinner was ready.

As soon as we sat down at the table Alex jumped in with a series of questions for Lani that seemed to encourage the others to join in the conversation as well. I felt myself begin to relax as the meal progressed and everyone got to know one another a bit better.

"If you live in Hawaii you must know how to surf," Scooter said to Luke.

"I do surf," Luke said, "although I'm not as good as Lani, who's a master on the waves."

"That's only because I was taught to surf almost before I could walk," Lani countered.

"So you were born in Hawaii?" Ellie asked.

"Yes. My family has lived on Oahu for many generations, and while some of my brothers have moved to other islands, the entire family still lives in Hawaii."

Ellie turned to Luke. "And I understand you're from Texas."

"I am. My family owns a ranch in the panhandle."

"A ranch!" Scooter almost jumped out of his chair. "Are you a real cowboy?"

Luke laughed. "I suppose I started out that way, but, unlike my brothers, I moved on to other things."

Poor Scooter looked disappointed. "Other things? What could be better than being a cowboy? Do you have a hat?"

"I do have a cowboy hat. Several, actually."

"Wow. Do you have boots and a gun too? Not a rifle; the kind the cowboys have in the movies, with a holster you wear around your hips while you're riding your horse in case someone tries to steal your cows."

Based on Scooter's expression, it seemed that in his mind being a cowboy was the best job on the planet.

Luke laughed again. "I have boots and a gun, but I don't usually wear the gun and I don't have cows. I have a horse, though. In fact, at the moment I have ten horses."

"Wow!"

"And other than yourself, does your entire family still live in Texas?" Ellie inquired after Scooter sat back down in his chair.

"They do. My parents own a ranch, as do my two older brothers, and both of my sisters are married to ranchers nearby. They all live within twenty miles of one another, which seems a little close to me, but they seem very happy. A lot of folks think of Texas as being a large dust bowl, but it's beautiful country, and those who are born and bred there tend to stick around."

"But you didn't," Scooter pointed out.

Luke took a sip of his wine before answering. "No. I guess I'm one of the few who suffer from wanderlust. I went to college after graduating high school and then moved to New York City, where I worked in the stock market for a while. When I'd had enough of that fast-paced lifestyle I quit and traveled for a couple of years before settling down on Oahu to breed horses."

Levi asked Luke about his time in New York, and then Zak asked about some of the places overseas they'd both visited. Ellie asked about the town where he grew up and Scooter launched into a long discourse about rodeos and bull riding. Everyone seemed to be enjoying the conversation, but when the topic turned to Luke's sisters and the babies they were both about to have, I noticed Lani begin to frown, so I decided to change the subject.

"We're having a big Easter dinner here on Sunday. I'd like you both to come if you aren't busy. With the exception of the photo my mom is planning to have taken of the immediate family, it'll be very informal. Just family and friends; good food and an egg hunt for the kids."

Luke glanced at Lani, who didn't answer, before offering a vague comment about letting me know after he and Lani had a chance to talk about it.

By the time dinner was over, Scooter had asked every question he could think of about being a cowboy, Zak and I had filled Luke and Lani in on our plans for Zimmerman Academy, Levi had told them about his job coaching at the high school, Ellie had shared some of the plans she had for the remodel, and Alex had talked about the plot of the book she was writing and hoped to have published.

Ellie served a delicious dessert, then announced she was tired and going to their suite to relax, and Levi joined her. Alex and Scooter headed up to their rooms and Zak and Luke went to check on the decryption program he was running, and Lani and I did the dishes.

"I'm sorry Scooter was so stuck on the whole cowboy thing," I said as I rinsed the dishes and stacked them into the dishwasher while Lani transferred the leftovers into plastic bowls. "We're working on his social skills, but he hasn't quite mastered the concept of conversational flow."

Lani began to put the leftovers into the refrigerator. "It's okay. He's a nice kid, and I can understand how a twelve-year-old boy would be more interested in cowboys, bull riding, and shoot-outs than jobs and decorating."

"I really appreciate how patient Luke was. Not all men would have taken the time to explain everything in such detail. It seems like you have yourself a pretty great guy."

Lani smiled. "Yeah, I really do."

I asked Lani about her job at the resort and she asked me about my work with wild and domestic animals. She was easy to talk to, and I found that we had a lot in common. When we finished in the kitchen we joined the men in the computer room, only to find Zak sitting in front of the screen with Luke standing behind him, looking over his shoulder. Zak had a particular expression on his face that I'd learned to equate to confusion or frustration, while Luke just looked curious.

"Did you find anything?" I asked as I came up behind Zak and put my hand on his shoulder.

"I'm not sure," he answered as he placed his hand over mine and gave it a squeeze.

I leaned over and looked at the screen. There were letters, numbers, and symbols in neat rows devoid of spaces that would indicate separations of words or phrases. I tried to make sense of what I was looking at, but it was just gibberish to me. After a brief silence, I said, "I guess you still haven't been able to decrypt it."

Zak shook his head. "No, but I'm close. I just need to figure out the best way to approach the problem." He flexed his fingers as he often did before he launched into a typing spree, so I took several steps back to allow him the room he'd need. Lani took a cue from me and took some steps back as well.

"Wow, he's really fast," Lani said as Zak typed so rapidly I could barely see his fingers on the keyboard.

Luke made a comment to Zak, but he didn't answer. I'd come across him in this state many times in the past and learned that when he was in the cyberzone he blocked out the rest of the world entirely. I informed Luke that it would be useless to try to talk to him until he came out of the zone of his own volition.

Luke turned and looked at Lani and me. "I get that. Concentration is key to tackling the sort of work Zak is engaged in."

After a good fifteen minutes Zak stopped typing. He sat back in his chair and looked at the screen before turning to me. "Get Alex," he finally said.

I nodded and ran upstairs to let Alex know Zak needed her assistance. She immediately jumped up and trotted down the stairs to the computer room. Zak took a moment to explain what he wanted her to do and she nodded and sat down at the computer to his left. Then he turned to Luke and gave him a similar yet slightly different set of instructions, and Luke sat down at a computer to Zak's right. He gave a signal and all three began to type.

"What are they doing?" Lani asked me in a voice just above a whisper. We stood to the back of the room so we wouldn't disturb them.

"I'm not sure," I answered. "All the computers in the room are linked to a central server and I've seen Alex and Zak together like this when they're working through a complicated hack, so I suppose Zak realized this particular code would need to be approached from different angles."

"Didn't you tell me Alex is twelve?" Lani asked with a look of amazement on her face as she watched her fingers flying across her keyboard.

"Alex is twelve, but she's a genius. She knows and understands more about pretty much everything than I ever will."

Lani continued to watch Alex as she worked. "That's amazing. I didn't even understand the instructions Zak gave her. It sounded like another language."

"It *was* another language: computer language."

"Not that it's any of my business, and you don't have to answer if you don't want to, but how exactly did Alex end up living here with you and Zak?"

I turned to Lani and began what was a long story I'd need to summarize. "We met Alex through Scooter, who grew up in Ashton Falls. After Scooter's mother died his father went off the deep end, leaving Scooter mostly unattended. To be honest, he was a real handful, in trouble more often than not. Zak, who has a huge heart, felt sorry for him and sort of took him under his wing."

"What a kind thing to do."

"I thought Zak was crazy at first. Scooter was like a human tornado, but Zak was patient and Scooter seemed to adore him, so eventually Zak was able to establish his role as an authority figure in Scooter's life and really helped to turn him around."

I took a deep breath before I continued. "Eventually, Zak realized Scooter needed a lot more supervision than he was getting at home, so he arranged to pay for Scooter to attend boarding school. That's where Scooter met Alex. Alex's parents are archeologists who travel a lot, and one Christmas he brought her home when he found out she was going to be alone."

"Home, as in your home?"

"Yes. By that point Scooter was pretty much living with us when he wasn't in school. Anyway, I fell in love with Alex immediately. She opened my mind and my heart in so many things. During one of her visits I found out that because she was already beyond the curriculum at their school her parents were planning to send her directly to high school. She was only ten! Alex is smart, but she's also a kid, and it would have been horrible for her socially. Zak arranged with Alex's parents for her to live with us and attend Zimmerman Academy. She's still the youngest student in the school, but she has a stable home life and a few friends closer to her age, so we feel she has a balance between being gifted academically and being a kid."

"It seems like you're doing a good job. She seems very happy and well adjusted."

"Thanks. That means a lot. We love Alex and Scooter like they're our own and want to do what's best for them in the long run."

"And Scooter? Does he attend Zimmerman Academy as well?" Lani asked.

"No. Scooter's special in his own way, but he's an average student. We thought the best place for him was public school, and he seems happy where he is and has several good friends. He sometimes talks about attending the Academy, so we may reconsider when we're able to admit younger kids. We currently have high school students with above average IQs, but Zak and I want to open things up to kids with a variety of talents."

Lani glanced at Alex, Luke, and Zak, still working away, then returned her attention to me. "How did you come up with the idea of opening the school in the first place?"

"Believe it or not, it came out of an almost-fight we had when his mother put our first child on the waiting list for an exclusive boarding school before we were even married."

Lani looked surprised. "Huh? I thought you didn't have children."

"We don't, but that didn't stop my mother-in-law. Her action, while it angered me, created an opening for Zak and me to discuss the situation. I made it perfectly clear that no child of mine was going to boarding school and Zak pointed out that many of the best schools were boarding. The reality is there's a good chance that our children, when we finally get around to having them, could have Zak's brain. It would be a waste to send a genius to an average public school, so we came up with the idea of starting our own school where our kids could live at home *and* have the best education money could buy."

Lani and I continued to chat quietly while the team worked together to crack the code. Every now and then Zak would bark out an instruction, but other than that the room was totally silent except for our whispering and the clicking of the keys as he and the others worked in tandem to find the answer they sought. After at least thirty minutes Zak stopped typing. "I got it," he shouted.

Alex and Luke stopped typing and turned to look at Zak's screen.

"Wow, that's unexpected," Alex said from her position at his side.

"Why in the world would Rossi encrypt this?" Luke agreed.

The thumb drive held not a message but a photo. A photo of a landscape that looked as if it could have been taken locally based on the scenery. The photo itself was unspectacular, featuring a forest with a path running through it and an old house that didn't look to be inhabitable in the background. The house looked vaguely familiar, but I couldn't place it offhand. There were ferns growing under the trees and in the far distance there was a filtered view of water that I assumed was a lake. The trees grew so densely, it was impossible to pick out any features that would distinguish the photo as having been taken of *our* forest and *our* lake rather than any other.

"Maybe there's a clue in the photo?" Lani suggested.

I squinted as I tried to focus on small sections of it at a time. "If there is, it's well hidden."

Zak pulled the photo up on the large screen that was mounted on the wall. It made the image easier to see, but if you asked me it still looked like a photo of trees, foliage, a path, and a lake. After the five of us had stared at it until we were cross-eyed we agreed to call it a night and pick up where we left off the next day.

After Luke and Lani left Zak and I drove to Will's house. It was dark and locked up tight. We knocked just in case, but there was no answer. I was starting to get worried about the guy.

Chapter 10

Saturday, April 15

The photo didn't really help us to understand exactly who had killed Charles Rossi, but I called Salinger before heading downstairs to breakfast with the rest of the family. Part of the agreement he and I had worked out over the years was that I would keep him updated on even the tiniest detail of whatever case we were working on.

"Where's Ellie?" I asked after pouring myself a cup of coffee and taking a seat at the table.

"Still in bed. She had another rough night." Levi sighed. "I hope this baby comes soon. I don't think the stress is good for her or Eli."

"Maybe you should talk to her doctor to see what he thinks," I suggested. Poor Levi looked both worried and exhausted.

"Ellie has an appointment this morning. Unless he says Eli will definitely be here within the next couple of days, I'll pull him aside to talk about what's going on. I've been to all of Ellie's appointments, and whenever he asks her how's she's doing she plasters on a smile and says she's great."

"That's Ellie for you. She isn't one to complain."

"Yeah. I can see she's really trying, but I know her well enough to tell she's really on edge. I hate to see her so angsty and uncomfortable. I wish I could take over and carry Eli for a while."

I tried for an encouraging smile. "This is hard on both of you. I'm sure it won't be long. In fact, I'm willing to bet you'll have a son by the end of the weekend."

Levi stood up and began making a plate for Ellie. "I hope so."

I scooped some of the egg casserole Zak had made onto a plate and added a piece of toast and two pieces of bacon after Levi headed down the hall with Ellie's food. I was about to bring up my plans for the day when Zak got a call and left the room to take it, leaving just Alex, Scooter, and me at the table.

"Do the two of you have plans for the day?" I asked.

"Me and Tucker are going to a movie. His aunt is taking us," Scooter announced. "I asked Zak and he said it was okay."

"A movie sounds like fun. Be sure to thank Tucker's aunt for taking you."

"I will."

I turned to Alex. "How about you? Any plans?"

"I'm going over to Phyllis's to work on my book." Alex referred to the principal of Zimmerman Academy, who was helping her publish the book she had been working on. "In fact, I should go get ready. She'll be here to pick me up in less than thirty minutes."

After Alex left the room I glanced back at Scooter. "Do you need a ride into town?"

"No. Tucker's aunt is coming to get me. I could use some money, though. I was going to ask Zak, but he's busy, so ..."

I smiled. "No problem. My purse is on my dresser. I have cash if you'll run up to get it. I want to eat before my food gets cold."

"Thanks, Zoe." Scooter pushed back his chair, put his dishes in the sink, and ran up the stairs.

I'd just taken my first bite of lukewarm eggs when Zak came back into the room. "That was Will," he announced. "It turns out he had gone camping and didn't have cell service, which is why he wasn't returning anyone's calls."

I let out a long breath of relief.

"He said he did have lunch with Charles Rossi, who asked him a bunch of questions about encrypting data and how to do it, but he didn't do any encrypting for him. When I explained what he'd used he agreed Rossi couldn't have done it himself but didn't have any idea who might have helped him. We discussed some possibilities and suggested the photo might have a hidden code that would only be visible under infrared light or possibly if the photo was inverted. I'm going to take a drive over to the Academy to check some things out. I won't be long; maybe a couple of hours. Come if you like, but I'm pretty sure you'll be bored."

I shook my head. "No, thanks. I have some errands to run to get ready for tomorrow. Text me when you're done and we can arrange to meet."

Zak left and I went upstairs to take a shower and dress. Zak had the food handled for the next day, but I wanted to buy items to make an Easter basket for each of the kids. Alex and Scooter were on the verge of being too old for such things, but something told me they'd still enjoy being included, so I'd need six baskets if I included Harper, Jeremy's daughter Morgan, his stepdaughter, Rosalie, and Tucker.

As I dried my hair, I thought about Will's suggestion that the photo might contain a code and realized it was likely it did. Otherwise going to the trouble of encrypting such an ordinary photo made no sense. If there was a code or some sort of message hidden in the photo I was confident Zak would find it, though I was less confident the photo would lead us to the identity of Rossi's killer and the treasure.

Pulling on my clothes, I considered the clues I hadn't yet followed up on. We still needed to find out how Charles Rossi had gotten into the lake, which meant a visit to the local marinas was paramount. I also needed to track down Mac Walters to see if he knew anything about the azurite Rossi was looking for, and I found the baby buggy incident odd enough that I felt a visit to both stores he had browsed in that day would be worth the effort. Perhaps I could multitask, fitting some sleuthing in with the shopping I needed to do anyway. I decided to start my expedition in the craft store, where the woman with the baby buggy had seen Rossi sorting through the blankets. It would be a good place to buy the baskets and ribbons I needed for the Easter baskets and I could interview the store owner while I shopped.

Luckily, there were only a few women browsing when I arrived. I grabbed a shopping basket, picked out some small baskets and ribbon for each of the children, and then headed to the checkout counter while there was no one in line.

"Morning, Eve," I greeted the tall woman behind the counter. I wouldn't say we were good friends and I wasn't the sort to buy craft supplies on a regular basis, but she'd lived in Ashton Falls for quite some time, so we were acquainted.

"Looks like you're planning on company," she said as she rang up the baskets. "It was smart to wait. These are buy-one, get-one-half-off today."

"Wonderful. And yes, we're having a small gathering tomorrow. I thought baskets would be nice for the kids."

"If you're going to do an egg hunt you might want to consider plastic eggs," Eve said. "They hold up better than real ones and if you miss one you don't have to worry about the smell."

"Good idea. Do you sell them?"

"We're out, but I know they had some at the five-and-dime. Did Ellie have her baby yet? The last time I saw her, she looked like she was ready to pop."

"No, not yet. But I should make up a basket for Eli. I'm sure Ellie would appreciate it."

"Run back and get what you need. I'll bag this stuff up while you're gone."

I hurried around the shop, picking up one more basket and another package of blue-checked ribbon. While I was at it I also grabbed some adorable stuffed bunnies for Eli and the younger kids. I'd get something more age appropriate for Alex, Scooter, and Tucker.

"I understand you had quite a bit of excitement in here earlier in the week," I said when I returned to the counter.

"Excitement?" Eve asked as she rang up the items I'd just gathered.

"Someone told me that visiting professor was looking through the baby buggy of one of your customers."

Eve waved a hand. "Oh, that. I wouldn't exactly call that excitement, but it was strange. At first I couldn't imagine what the man was doing, but when I thought about it after he left I was fairly certain I saw him take something out of the buggy and slip it under his jacket. I asked the woman if she was missing anything and she said she wasn't, so it occurred to me that perhaps he'd stolen something from the shop they both were in before this one and he'd used the buggy to sneak it out."

I frowned. "Why would he do that? I mean, he was a professor."

Eve shrugged. "It takes all kinds. Now and then I see reports on the news of someone with a whole lot more money than I'll ever have caught shoplifting. Some folks just have a sickness, it seems."

I supposed that was true. I'd heard on more than one occasion of a wealthy actress stealing makeup or clothing. But Charles Rossi? He'd seemed too distinguished for that. Besides, what would the consignment shop have that he would want? I decided that would be my next stop.

The consignment shop sold a little bit of everything and didn't seem to be organized in much of a logical manner, which made browsing, when you weren't in a hurry, so potentially interesting. Today, however, I didn't have time for that, so I went straight to the counter and said hello to the cashier, who, like Eve, I knew only casually.

"Zoe, how are you?" she asked.

"I'm good. And yourself?"

"Not bad," the short, plump blonde replied. "Are you looking for something special today?"

"No. I actually just had a question for you about a man who was in the shop earlier in the week."

The clerk glanced at me with knowing eyes. She leaned forward and lowered her voice. "Are you asking about the man who turned up dead? I knew you'd be looking into that."

I nodded. "Yes. Do you remember him being in the store?"

"I absolutely do. He stood out right away. It's not often that distinguished-looking men in tweed jackets stop by to browse."

"Did he seem interested in anything specific?" I wondered.

She tilted her head to the side, considering my question. "Yes and no. He didn't ask for help nor did he accept any when I offered. And he didn't pause too long over any one item. But he didn't seem to be browsing casually either. He looked like a man on a mission, I'm just not sure what he was looking for, or if he ever found it."

I crossed my arms on the counter and leaned forward. "Did you hear that he was caught looking through a woman's baby buggy over at the craft shop?"

"I did hear that. Eve thought maybe he'd stolen something from me and used the buggy to sneak it out. As far as I can tell, nothing's missing. The idea that he might have used the buggy to sneak something out isn't a bad theory, though. In fact, I think that's most likely exactly what happened."

"I thought you weren't missing anything." I looked around the cluttered shop and wondered how she'd even know if she was, but I didn't say as much.

"I'm not; I think he slipped something into the buggy he already had on him."

I narrowed my gaze. "Like what?"

"I'm not sure. I didn't actually see him drop anything into the buggy, but a man walked in while he was here, looked around, and the professor sort of frowned. They made eye contact, and then the second man left. And the professor passed close by the baby buggy on his way out the door."

"Was the baby in the buggy?" I asked.

"No. The baby was fussy, so the mom was holding him. I didn't think anything about the whole thing until I heard about what happened over at the craft store. If you ask me the professor wanted to be sure to hide something from the other man who came in."

That was an interesting theory. Unfortunately, the clerk didn't know who the second man was for sure, though she said that, when asked, one of the other customers thought his name might have been Tim or Tom and he worked for the county. The county offices were only open until noon today, so I'd have to hurry if I wanted to check it out. I asked for a description of the man, but all she could remember was average height, short dark hair, wearing jeans and a blue T-shirt.

We talked for a few more minutes, then I exited the store and headed to the county building, which was close enough to walk to. There was a man with a small mouth and beady eyes behind the counter with a name badge that identified him as Tom Cobalter.

"We'll be closing in five minutes," he said the moment I walked in the door. He clearly wasn't interested in having someone come in at the last minute who might keep him late.

"I just have a quick question," I assured him. "I want to know whether a man named Charles Rossi has been in here this week looking for information."

He frowned before answering. "No. That name doesn't ring a bell. Any particular reason you're asking?"

I thought I'd noticed a flash of something in his eyes before he answered, but I couldn't be sure. "Charles was a friend," I said. "He passed away this week and I was following up on some research he was doing for a book he was writing."

He seemed to relax visibly. "Yeah, I heard about that, but he never came in here and spoke to me. I suppose if he intended to he hadn't gotten around to it."

"Okay." I smiled. "Thank you for your help."

I left the office and returned to my car, turning things over in my mind. The man hadn't said anything suspicious, but I had a feeling he hadn't been as forthright as he'd tried to make himself appear. If he didn't want to share what he knew I couldn't force him to talk; I headed to Donovan's to stock up on candy and other trinkets for the baskets. My dad was off all weekend, so I imagined one of the two women he employed would be at the counter today.

The first thing I noticed upon entering the store, which sold a little bit of a lot of things, was Lani chatting with Dad's newest hire, Amanda Urbine.

"Lani, what are you doing here?" I asked as I approached the counter.

"I was out running some errands and wanted to stop in to check out your dad's store. It's charming, by the way. So quaint and cozy."

"Thank you. I'll tell him you said so. Is Luke with you?"

"No, he's back at the cabin. He had some work to do on the computer, so I decided to take advantage of the alone time to check out the town. Is Zak with you?"

"He's at the Academy, taking a closer look at the photo we found."

"I'm sorry to interrupt," Amanda said, "but as long as you're here," she looked at me, "can you cover the register for a few minutes so I can take a quick break?"

"Absolutely. Take all the time you need." I turned my attention back to Lani. "As I was saying, Zak took the photo to the Academy, where he could use the larger computers to look for hidden clues."

"I sure didn't notice anything last night," Lani commented.

"Me neither, but he thought maybe the photo needed to be manipulated in some way to expose whatever might be hidden."

"I guess that makes sense. Do you have any news?"

"Not really. After I get what I need here I'm going to check out the marinas on this end of the lake. It's possible Rossi was dumped from a private boat, but it wouldn't hurt to inquire about rentals. There aren't a lot of boats rented out this time of year, so it should be easy to eliminate this possibility."

"I'll come with you, if you don't mind some company," Lani offered. "I'm about done with my shopping for the day."

I smiled. "I'd love some company."

We headed out when Amanda returned, taking my car and leaving Lani's rental in the parking lot.

The first two marinas we visited turned out to be dead ends, but the third had rented out a boat that seemed like a real possibility. It had been out for a week, beginning two days before the morning Lani found Rossi's body. The boat was a cabin cruiser that summertime visitors rented to float around the lake while partying. It was currently docked in the marina, but the guy at the rental counter said the man who'd rented it had a couple more days left on his short-term lease. I asked him to point it out, thanked him, and we headed out to the parking area.

"I'd love to get a look inside that boat," I said to Lani.

"I was thinking the same thing."

I looked around but didn't see anyone either on the deck of the boat or loitering nearby. We discussed it and decided to casually approach the boat; if someone was on board we'd simply say we'd mistaken the boat for the one friends had rented and be on our way.

"Hello," I yelled as we approached.

Lani and I waited for a few seconds, but there was no reply. We quietly stepped onto the boat, then quickly made our way to the door to the cabin.

"Hello," I called again as I opened the door. I was met with silence. I glanced at Lani, who nodded, and we made our way to the seating area, where there were computers set up. There were rows of bunks toward the rear of the seating area as well as a very small kitchen to the right and an even smaller bathroom to the left.

The boat looked like it would sleep six, a typical size for the boats on the lake. If Rossi had been dumped from this boat—

and my Zodar told me he had—I hoped we'd be able to find some sort of evidence of it.

"Look around for blood or any signs of a struggle," I suggested. "I assume Rossi was hit while on the deck before being tossed overboard, but we can't know that for certain."

"Don't you think it's strange that whoever tossed him in the lake didn't take his life vest off first?" Lani asked.

I agreed it did. Had it been me disposing of the body, I would have found a way to weight it so it wouldn't have been discovered so easily. "Maybe there was a struggle and he fell overboard," I mused. "There would have been fishing boats in the area at that time of the morning, so whoever he fought with wouldn't want to make a big production of rescuing him only to dump him again."

Lani lifted the cushion of one of the chairs in the seating area. "That makes as much sense as anything. It might even be possible whoever Rossi struggled with didn't mean to kill him. They could have been fighting over one thing or another when Rossi fell over the railing, hitting his head as he fell toward the water."

"That's a good theory. Let's check the railing for blood."

I was just about to go through the door that led from the cabin to the deck when I saw two men approaching the boat. I jumped back inside. "Someone's coming. We need to hide."

Lani glanced around. "There's too much space between the bottom of the bunks and the floor. We'd most likely be spotted. It looks like the only place to hide is in the cabinets near the bunks. I hope they're empty."

Chapter 11

We hurried to the back of the cabin and opened the first cabinet, which was filled with climbing equipment. We'd opened the second just as I heard the first man step onto the deck. It was empty, so we both squeezed inside. It was a good thing we were both petite; there was no way two average-size adults would have fit in that cramped space. We stood in the dark as quietly as we could. I prayed the men were just there to drop something off and would leave again immediately. My hopes were dashed the moment I heard one tell the other to shove off.

"Do you want a beer?" The man, who was still in the cabin and sounded a lot like Owen Gallo from Outback Hunting and Fishing, had called to the one who was on the deck. I couldn't hear his reply over the sound of the engine, but I imagined he'd declined the offer because I could hear the man in the cabin doing something in the small kitchen. Based on the sound of cabinets opening and closing, I thought he was making something to eat. I hoped he'd head up to the deck when he was done, allowing Lani and me time to regroup. Not only was the cabinet dark, it was an incredibly tight fit, making for a very uncomfortable and fairly intimate hiding place. Of course trying to sneak out and taking the risk of exposing ourselves wasn't really an option, so I simply sucked in my stomach as far as I could and waited for whatever was going to happen.

My heart was pounding as I considered all the possible outcomes to the current scenario. The best one to my mind was that one of the men would say something that would indicate they weren't the killers I suspected them of being, and Lani and I could reveal ourselves and be returned to the marina after a brief, awkward exchange that would look a lot like an episode from the sitcom playing through my head entitled *Oops, I Seem to Have Stumbled onto the Wrong Boat.* The second-best was that the men were traveling to another marina, where they would dock and leave and we'd be able to sneak away after a short but uncomfortable ride. A slightly worse scenario was that we'd remain undiscovered but the trip would be longer, followed by the worst case, which had one or both of the men opening the cabinet with guns drawn to reveal our hiding place.

It was dark in the cabinet and I couldn't make out Lani's features, although I was close enough to kiss her. In fact, her hair was brushing my face, creating an almost uncontrollable urge to brush it away, but as long as one man remained below deck it was too risky to move or speak. So we remained chest to chest and waited. I could hear the man in the kitchen talking, although he wasn't yelling to be heard by the one on deck, so I assumed he was speaking to someone on the phone. Either that or there was a third man involved rather than just the two. I listened intently, trying to make out what he was saying. The engine was loud, drowning out most of what he said, but I was pretty sure I caught the words *nosy lady*. Great. What were the odds they were referring to me?

After a few minutes I heard him head up to the deck. We waited at least another minute to make sure he wasn't going to come back before opening the door to the cabinet just a crack, which offered a very limited view. So I opened the door a tiny bit more.

"I think they're both on the deck," I whispered.

"We should call for help," Lani suggested.

I looked at my phone. In the place where lines usually were displayed it said *no service*. "I'll check again in a minute. The lake has pockets without service; most of the time service goes in and out as you travel."

"What now?" Lani asked. "Should we try to sneak into position to hear what they're talking about?"

I considered. I wanted to know what they had planned, but if we left the cabinet and ventured into the seating area we'd be exposed if one of the men decided to come below deck. "I don't think we can risk it. At least not yet. Maybe this will be a short trip and we'll be out of here soon."

At least with the cabinet door cracked open we had a little light as well as fresh air. "Did you catch anything the man was saying?" I whispered to Lani.

"Not much. He seemed to be annoyed that someone had been asking around about Charles Rossi and his death, and he mentioned something about an island."

I opened my eyes wide. "The lake has only one island. Oh my gosh, I should have realized." I rolled my eyes as I kicked myself mentally.

"Realized what?" Lani asked, obviously wondering what I was so upset about.

"The island of the blue stone. That has to be where the treasure is hidden."

"Azurite," Lani remembered.

"I'm not sure if the stone is really azurite. It might be. What I do know is that, while the island is deserted now, at one time a long time ago a woman lived on it in near isolation for nearly sixty years."

"She lived there alone?" Lani whispered.

I nodded. "She came to Devil's Den with her husband, who was a miner. He died in a terrible accident and everyone thought she'd leave, go back to the East Coast, where she came from, but instead she hired some men to build her a house on the island, where she lived alone until she died. The only real contact she had with the outside world was the supply boat that brought her whatever she required once a week. I remember when I was in grade school the teacher telling us this story, and one of my classmates asked how she paid for the supplies if she didn't have a job. The teacher said she paid for what she needed with the blue stone found on the island. That must be the blue stone referred to in the journal."

Lani put a hand over my mouth and pulled me deeper into the cabinet, closing the door as she did so. I frowned, but then heard someone entering the cabin.

"Yeah, hang on," the man I thought was Owen Gallo called to the one still up on the deck. Lani and I both held our breath so we wouldn't make a noise. I felt my heart almost leap out of my chest as I heard the door of the cabinet next to the one in which we were hiding open. Then the door slammed closed and I saw our cabinet door begin to open just as something fell with a loud boom.

I let out a slow but silent breath as the man cussed and the door closed. I could hear him rooting around outside the cabinet and assumed we'd been granted a temporary reprieve when something else from the next cabinet fell on the floor. Of course once he cleaned things up chances were he'd return his attention to this cabinet. I laced my fingers through Lani's and gave her hand a gentle squeeze. She squeezed back. It took all my strength to remain silent as the man worked just outside our hiding place.

"Did you find it?" the man on the deck called down.

"Not yet," the man outside our cabinet called back.

"Look in the last cabinet."

My heartbeat slowed just a bit as I realized the last cabinet wasn't ours.

"Got it," the man called back and then headed back to the deck.

I heard Lani exhale. "That was close."

"Too close," I agreed.

"Do you think there's a better hiding place?" Lani whispered.

"I don't know. I didn't see one when we were in the cabin earlier, but we didn't have much time to look around. If we're headed to the island we should be there in about fifteen minutes. I think it might be best to wait it out and hope they don't need anything else from the cabinets."

"Agreed."

Lani and I fell into silence. My mind was working rapidly, trying to come up with a plan for when we arrived at the island. I cracked the door open just a tiny bit to let in some light and fresh air. I looked at my phone. Damn; there was still no service.

"If you send a text it will be stored in the phone's memory and whenever it gets service it'll send, even if you aren't aware of it," Lani said.

"That's a good idea. Let's both send a text. Maybe one of them will go through. And even if they don't, I'm sure Zak will figure out a way to save us. He always does."

"This kind of thing happens to you often?"

I smiled. "More often than I like to admit. It's kind of our thing; I get into trouble and Zak saves me."

Lani narrowed her eyes. "And that doesn't bother you?"

I paused before answering. "I suppose in the beginning I had this idea that I should be taking care of myself, but it didn't take long for me to realize I'm better and stronger as part of a team. I don't know that it was intentional on either of our parts, but by this point Zak and I have established a routine. We're partners. I get into trouble and Zak saves me; it's just the way things work."

Lani frowned, but before she could say anything more the door was ripped wide open and we were face-to-face with Owen Gallo.

Chapter 12

All I could manage was to stare at him with my mouth hanging open and pray that I had somehow developed the gift of invisibility. I closed my eyes and willed him to close the door and move on, but that wasn't to be.

"Well, well, well," the man drawled with a gleam in his eye. "Look what the cat dragged in. Are the two of you comfy in there?"

"Very comfy," Lani said in such a nonchalant way that it seemed to mask the fear I knew she must be feeling. "Is the cruise over already? It seems much too soon. I did, after all, pay for the full stowaway experience."

Gallo grinned. "I like you. You have moxie. I just hope I don't have to kill you."

"If you don't want to kill us, don't," Lani reasoned as Gallo pulled first her and then me into the narrow space between the bunks and the cabinets. "In fact, if you want to pretend you never saw us I'm sure we can work with that."

He laughed. "I'm sorry, but these things are not up to me, little girl. We'll need to see how tolerant the boss is of stowaways. Based on what I know of him, I don't think he is going to be thrilled with your unscheduled visit."

Great. I was hoping he was the one in charge. He really did seem to like Lani and I'd hoped we could work that to our advantage. Lani held her head high as he shoved her into the seating area. I had to admire the girl's grit. It would seem having five older brothers had helped to make her tougher than her appearance would indicate.

"Hey, Tom," he yelled up to the deck. "Seems we have a couple of stowaways."

"Stowaways? What do you mean by stowaways?"

He held out a hand. "After you, ladies."

Lani went first and I fell in behind. We walked slowly to the deck where a man was dropping an anchor just off the island. When I realized Gallo's Tom was Tom from the county I wanted to kick myself for not following up and taking a closer look at him. If nothing else, his beady eyes should have tipped me off that he was up to no good.

His lips twisted as he looked Lani and me up and down. "Now where in tarnation have the two of you been all this time?"

"A cabinet," Gallo answered when neither of us spoke.

Tom glanced at Lani but glared at me. "I should have known you'd be sticking your nose where it doesn't belong. Seems to me you've developed a reputation for being a pest of the most annoying kind."

"Did you kill Charles Rossi?" I demanded. Even I knew it was an unwise question given the situation; still, if the man planned to kill us I may as well assuage my curiosity before he did it.

"Nobody killed Charles Rossi," he said, looking from me to Lani and then to Owen Gallo, as if he felt it was important to keep an eye on everyone. "The fool turned out to be nothing more than a menace to the project, and he certainly didn't have any business being on a boat. We hit one tiny bump and he fell overboard, hitting his head on the way to the water."

"If he fell and wasn't pushed you could have pulled him back into the boat," I pointed out.

"Yup," he said. "I suppose we could have, but when life offers you an opportunity, I figure it's your responsibility to take it."

"Opportunity?"

"When the professor first came to me with questions about historical permits and land ownership I was intrigued. I got him to open up, share the reason he was asking, and realized I was looking at a golden opportunity. Rossi had the journal, but he didn't know the area and couldn't follow the clues. I had a historical perspective, and my position with the county provided me access to private property and secure documents. Gallo here had the climbing skills we felt we'd need."

"So you got him to agree to a partnership," I inserted.

"Of sorts. Although it turned out the professor didn't plan to keep the treasure once he found it. The fool actually wanted to find the loot and return it to the rightful owners, whoever that might be. Can you imagine? The man didn't have a lick of sense, if you ask me."

I remembered the odd behavior Rossi had exhibited at the craft and consignment stores. He must have held back a valuable piece of information from his partners. They'd realized it and begun following him. I wondered if they'd ever talked him out of whatever they were looking for; given the fact that we were anchored beside the island where I figured the treasure must be, I had to assume that, in the end, they'd gotten what they were after.

"So you let him drown?" I said, anger evident in my voice.

Cobalter shrugged. "Like I said, I'm not one to turn down an opportunity when it presents itself. I'm not sure I could actually have killed the professor, but turning a blind eye and pretending I didn't see him fall overboard was easier than I expected."

I glanced at Lani, who appeared to be clamping her mouth shut, I was certain, in an effort not to say something that would make the situation worse.

"What do you want to do with them?" Gallo asked after a brief pause.

Cobalter hesitated. Then he turned to look at the island behind him. "You know, this might work out just fine. Put them in the dinghy and take them ashore. Get their phones first, though, and toss them in the lake."

I was about to protest before I glanced at Gallo; for the first time I noticed he had a gun. If the texts Lani and I had loaded hadn't sent yet there was no way they would now. She gave me a brief nod, as if to communicate that she too had figured we should cooperate at this point.

After we were on the dinghy we were taken to the island, where we were seated on logs facing each other. Our hands and feet were tied and secured to the logs but not gagged. Of course there was no one around to hear us scream and I assumed the men knew that. I watched as Gallo returned for supplies. I couldn't imagine what was going to happen next.

"What do you think he meant by our being here working out just fine?" Lani asked, tossing her head in Cobalter's direction.

I looked around. "I don't know, but I have a feeling we aren't going to like it. Can you loosen your ropes at all?"

Lani wiggled her arms. "No. Gallo knows his way around a knot. How about you?"

I shook my head.

"Do you think the texts went through before our phones went into the lake?" Lani asked.

"I have no idea." I took a deep breath and let it out slowly. "Either way, Zak will find us."

Lani gave me a serious look. "You really believe that?"

"With all my heart."

Lani didn't say anything more.

I could hear the men returning and assumed we'd find out soon enough what they had planned. The fact that Cobalter had as much as admitted he probably wouldn't have been able to kill Charles Rossi and Gallo seemed to have a thing for Lani could work in our favor. Perhaps they'd simply dig up the treasure and leave us here to fend for ourselves. Sure, being stranded on an island in the middle of the lake wasn't ideal, especially when no one could know where we were unless one of the texts happened to have gone through, but it was better than the alternative, which in my mind involved a confrontation with Gallo's gun.

They rechecked the ropes binding our hands and feet and told us to stay put, then continued toward the center of the island. If Peter Romanov had hidden his treasure on this island in 1917 the woman who'd lived on the island might have already been here. Of course I wasn't always the best student and really hadn't been paying attention to the story my teacher told, so it was probably just as likely the woman had come to the island after that. If the woman was already here she may have agreed to guard the treasure while he was in the hospital. If that had been the case the things Romanov had taken from Russia may have been hidden in the house. I hadn't been on the island since I was a child, but I remembered the house still standing then.

After Romanov died the woman could have sold off the treasure a piece at a time to help pay for her hermit lifestyle. If that was what had occurred, there wouldn't be a treasure left to find. How mad would that make Gallo and his beady-eyed partner? I preferred not to be the one on whom they took out their angst.

"Where do you think they went?" Lani asked after a moment.

"I suppose they want to find the treasure. It's occurred to me that if it was hidden on this island when the woman who built her home here, she may have sold it off years ago."

Lani narrowed her gaze. "I don't suppose that will bode well for us."

"Probably not," I agreed.

"If they're gone long enough I may be able to get out of these ropes," she said. "I've been using the bark on the log for cutting, and slowly but surely I can feel the rope around my hands begin to fray."

"That's a good idea." I began rubbing the rope around my own hands on the log I was tied to.

"How far is this island from the nearest land?" Lani asked.

I gave it some thought. "I guess if you walk around to the south end the nearest land is about a mile away."

"I've been trying to come up with a plan for getting off the island if they leave us here. It seemed like we came pretty far from the west shore, but if there's land a mile away on the south end I can totally do that."

I raised a brow. "You plan to swim a mile in icy water?"

Lani shrugged. "If I have to. I realize the water temperature is a problem, but the marathon swims I competed in ranged from five to ten kilometers."

Wow; color me impressed. I considered myself to be fit and strong, but I had nowhere near the physical prowess Lani did. Of course I hadn't been training for most of my life to show up my five older brothers.

"It sounds like they're coming back," Lani whispered.

I stopped working my ropes. If they were just stopping by to check on us maybe they wouldn't notice the progress

I'd made. I sat perfectly still and watched as they approached. I gasped when Gallo took out a long knife. I couldn't help but flinch when he walked around behind me. I sucked in a deep breath when he used the knife to cut the ropes tying my hands. He didn't say anything about the ropes being frayed. I wasn't certain whether it was because I hadn't made all that much progress or that he didn't care. He cut the ropes around my feet as well, then went over to Lani to cut her ropes.

I noticed it was now Cobalter who had the gun. Personally, I felt better about Gallo being the one with the weapon and hoped the two would exchange roles once the ropes were cut. Gallo seemed somewhat more stable; Cobalter looked like someone who would shoot first and ask questions later.

Cobalter motioned to Lani and me to walk down an overgrown trail. I took the lead, with Lani following closely behind. The men didn't speak while we walked, but given the fact that we were heading inland, I assumed we were heading toward the house, or what remained of it, stood. It wasn't long before the structure came into view, and Cobalter steered us to a wooden doorway that was low to the ground and looked as if it might lead to a root cellar or even a storm shelter.

Gallo lifted the heavy wooden door to reveal a dark hole. I couldn't see the bottom from where I stood, nor could I see stairs, but based on the narrowness of the opening I decided the hole wasn't a shelter as I'd first imagined.

"Is the treasure down there?" I asked.

"We think so," Gallo answered.

"That's a pretty narrow opening," I pointed out. "Do you think you can squeeze through?"

He smiled. "Don't need to." He glanced at Lani. "That's what we have your Spider-Man friend for."

"Wait," I yelled as Gallo tied a rope around Lani's waist and instructed her to sit on the ground with her feet dangling over the edge. "I'll do it. I can go down and look for the treasure." This was, after all, my town and therefore my case. I felt I should be the one taking whatever risk there might be.

"Don't worry." Gallo chuckled. "There will be enough fun to go around."

I sucked in a deep breath as Lani was lowered into the darkness. The men didn't seem to know how deep the hole was, and as they lowered her, they engaged in a conversation about having enough rope.

Finally the tension on the rope eased, indicating that Lani was on the bottom.

"What do you see?" Cobalter called down to her.

"It's dark. I can't see anything."

"Untie the rope from your waist," he instructed. "I'll lower down a flashlight."

I imagine Lani must have hesitated because the next thing I knew he was threatening to shoot me in the head if Lani didn't do as he said. Lani must have complied because the rope loosened even more and Cobalter pulled it up. He attached a large flashlight and lowered it down to her. Then he demanded to know what she saw and Lani yelled back that there was a small passage, barely large enough for her to squeeze through. Either Peter Romanov had been a tiny man or the tunnel had caved in, causing it to narrow. Or it could be the treasure wasn't hidden here at all.

I hated waiting. Not that I envied Lani and her trek into the dark unknown. But I wasn't used to sitting on the sidelines; the entire situation didn't sit well with me. I stood perfectly still, considering what to do. If the men intended to find the treasure and then let Lani and me go cooperating would be the best bet. If, however, they intended to find the treasure and kill us, as I suspected, I needed to make my move. I tried not to appear obvious as I looked around at my surroundings. I needed a weapon, but what was available to me that would compete with the gun Cobalter had tucked into his belt?

After a moment I heard Lani's voice. She had to yell to be heard. She said she'd found a room, or possibly a storage area, at the end of the tunnel that was separated from where she stood by a door with a lock that had rusted shut. Cobalter cursed; Gallo just looked amused by the whole thing. There was some discussion about Gallo trying to climb down to help Lani with the door, but a glance at the opening was enough to convince both men that his broad shoulders would never fit through. Cobalter was much slimmer and might be able to squeeze into the opening with added force from above, but his face had gone pale and I realized the toad was afraid of the dark. Finally they decided to send me down with the knife Gallo had used to cut away our ropes. I wasn't sure we'd be able to pry open the door with the knife, but I was done with standing around while Lani took all the risks and didn't put up a fight as they tied the rope around my waist and lowered me into the darkness.

The worst parts were the places along the way down where the passage was so small that my face scraped against the dirt and the pressure squeezed my chest so hard I found I couldn't breathe. Lani is a bit flatter-chested than I, and there were spots when I was sure I would be stuck. When I neared the bottom Lani grabbed my feet and pulled me into the only slightly larger chamber where she was waiting. I hugged her as best I could in the small space.

"Did you make it?" Cobalter called down.

"I made it," I yelled back.

"Okay, then, go pry open the door. When you get it open one of you needs to come back to the opening to let us know. We'll give you further instructions depending on what you find behind the door."

"Okay," Lani called. She took my hand and led me down the dark, narrow passage.

"Cobalter gave me his knife," I said from close behind Lani as we walked one behind the other. "I don't know if it'll be enough to pry the door open."

She stopped and pulled me into a part of the passage where the walls were somewhat wider. There was enough room for her to turn to face me. "There's no door," she whispered.

"What do you mean, there's no door?" I whispered back.

"The tunnel opens up to a closet at the back of the house. I used the rusted lock excuse to buy time, and to get them to send you down. Maybe we can get out of the house through a window and make our escape."

I paused to think. "Escape to where? We're on an island."

Lani shrugged. "We'll swim for it."

I certainly wasn't a distance swimmer, but I was in good shape, so I figured there was at least a 10 percent possibility that I wouldn't drown, although I wasn't certain about the hypothermia.

"Look, I know a mile sounds far, but it isn't. I know you said you run. Have you ever run a marathon?"

"Yeah. A couple."

"And what's the secret to finishing?" Lani asked me.

I thought about it. "It's really a mental game. You just have to keep going."

Lani smiled. "Exactly. Swimming is the same; you just have to keep on going. The water is cold, but the exertion of the swim will keep us warm. If you get into trouble

I'll save you. I'm a lifeguard, after all," Lani reminded me.

I wasn't a huge fan of the plan, but it was the only one we had, and I had no idea whether Zak would be able to find us before Cobalter shot us. If the texts had gone through help would have been here by now; I had to assume they hadn't.

"Okay," I agreed. "I'll go back to tell them the door lock is being stubborn, but we're working on it. That will buy us more time to make our escape."

"Okay. Take the flashlight. I'll wait here."

I headed back to the opening and called up to the men. I told them the lie we'd chosen, adding that I'd be back once we got the door open; then I hurried back to where Lani was waiting in the dark. We quietly made our way through the passage, then climbed up makeshift stairs to the opening in the bedroom closet, praying the whole time the men wouldn't decide to check out the house while they were waiting. We pulled ourselves through the opening as quietly as we could and headed to the window. The house had been built on a slope, so the distance to the ground from the window was close to two stories, but there was a tree close by. All that was required was a small leap to the closest branch and then a quick climb down.

Once we were on the ground we made our way through the forest as quietly as possible. It wasn't far, but I found I was sweating profusely from both physical effort and nerves. We stripped down to our underwear, hid our clothes in the brush, and waded into the freezing water for what would be the longest swim of my life.

I could tell Lani was holding back a bit in terms of speed, but I was happy to find that once I settled into a rhythm I kept up just fine. I thought we might make it until I heard the men shouting in the distance and bullets landing in the water all around us.

"Swim faster," Lani shouted.

I did, and the bullets stopped. I was under no illusion that we were out of danger. I realized the men probably had gone for the boat.

Lani and I swam at a steady pace, knowing Cobalter and Gallo would catch up to us at any time. Really, at this point there was little else we could do but swim. Returning to the island wasn't an option and there was nowhere to hide. The only chance we had was if the men decided we weren't a threat to their plan and let us be while they continued to look for the treasure.

I thought of Zak and my heart squeezed in pain as I considered the agony he would suffer when he learned I had died. I thought of Alex and Scooter, who once again would be without a mother figure, and Charlie, who might possibly suffer the most in my absence because he wouldn't understand why I hadn't come home.

My tears mingled with the water as I swam harder and faster than I ever had in my life. Ellie's face flashed into my mind and my heart ached at the thought that I'd never meet Baby Eli. I swam harder as anger took over, giving me endurance I'd never known I had. There were people in my life who depended on me. I had to find a way to survive.

Maybe it was the cold causing delusions, but I suddenly felt strong and confident that we'd make it. I knew I was going to live.

And then I heard the faint sound of a boat engine getting closer and closer.

I used the last of my strength to dig down deep and pick up speed. I kept going, more tears mingling with lake water until the moment I felt the boat pull up beside me. Strong arms reached into the water and pulled me out as the last of my strength faded.

I struggled against my captor until his voice penetrated my consciousness.

"Zak?" I fell into his arms, sobbing as he wrapped a blanket around me. "I knew you'd come."

Chapter 13

Thankfully, Zak had figured out what was going on and had, as I'd expected, come to rescue us. Luke was with him, and based on the look of love mixed with relief on Lani's face, I had a feeling her days of not wanting to be rescued were behind her. By the time Salinger made it to the island Owen Gallo and Tom Cobalter were long gone. Salinger called all the marinas, so there wasn't anywhere for the men to go. This was, after all, a lake, so there were only so many places to dock. Chances were they'd be behind bars by the end of the day.

"How did you guys know where we were?" Lani asked later that afternoon as the four of us sat around the fire pit Zak had built into our back deck.

"The hidden code in the photo revealed that the treasure was on the island," Zak explained as he held me on his lap and stroked my hair. "When Zoe wasn't home and wasn't answering her cell I figured she'd somehow managed to figure out the location of the treasure and gone after it on her own. I called Luke and we came running. It was a good thing we had an early spring; I'd already taken our boat out of storage. We might not have made it if we'd had to round up a boat first."

"Well, I can't thank you enough," Lani said. "I have to admit it was getting pretty dicey there at the end."

Zak shrugged. He looked deeply into my eyes and slid a finger down my cheek. "No thanks are necessary. Saving Zoe when her incredible sleuthing skills get her into trouble is kind of my thing."

Zak leaned forward and kissed me, and for a moment the world faded away.

******

Later that evening, after Luke and Lani had returned to their cabin, Zak and I were cuddled together in our big bed with a wall of pillows behind us. I was totally drained and exhausted and yet strangely invigorated. Salinger had called to let me know he'd tracked down both Cobalter and Gallo, who were both in jail. They didn't have the treasure in their possession; as far as he could tell, they'd never found it. I wasn't sure if it was still on the island or had been moved or sold off long ago, but Zak and I decided to go back to the island with Ethan, Luke, Lani, and the journal after the holiday to take another look around. It would be a fun outing among friends, though my intuition told me the treasure was long gone and we wouldn't find anything. I supposed in a way that might be for the best.

"I think we might need to work on our timing," Zak said as he ran a finger down my arm. My head rested on his chest and I could hear his heart beating beneath my ear.

"Timing?"

Zak kissed the top of my head. "I almost had a heart attack when I realized you and Lani had tried to swim for it. If we had gotten there sooner maybe we could have prevented that from happening."

"Or you and Luke might have gotten shot if you'd landed on the island. Tom Cobalter did have a gun," I reminded my strong and perfect husband. "And I know it seems like attempting to swim from the island to the beach sounds foolish, but Lani said I could do it, and you know, I think I could have. I'm in pretty good shape and I have a lot of physical endurance. Lani told me all I needed to do was keep swimming and I was doing pretty well until the bullets started flying."

"So about this physical endurance..." Zak smiled as he shifted and pulled me under him.

I wrapped my arms around his neck and was pulling his lips down to mine when there was a loud pounding on the door.

"It's time," I heard Levi yelled. "Ellie's having the baby."

Chapter 14

Sunday, April 16

What is there about Easter and babies? My sister Harper had been born three years ago on the day before Easter and Baby Eli Donovan Denton had made his appearance in the world at seven minutes after midnight on Easter day itself. He was a big, beautiful baby weighing in at nine pounds, seven ounces, with his father's thick, dark hair and deep blue eyes and his mother's huge, infectious smile. Not that newborns are supposed to be able to smile, but as I watched him sleeping in the bassinet next to his mother in her private hospital room, he looked up at me, and I chose to believe it was a genuine show of affection, not just gas as Alex insisted.

Ellie's labor had been short and Baby Eli was strong and healthy, so they planned to come home later that day.

"I think Harper has more egg dye on her dress than she does on her egg," I said to my mom, who had been smart enough to bring old clothes for my sister to change in to once we'd taken the family photos.

"Purple is her favorite color. Is Jeremy bringing Morgan and Rosalie?"

"He called to say they're running late, but the entire Fisher family should be here soon. And Grandpa and Hazel should be here within the hour. I figured once everyone got here we'd let the kids hunt for the plastic eggs filled with goodies that Zak and I got up early to hide."

Mom knelt next to Harper and wiped her purple-stained hands with a rag. "I'm surprised after yesterday's ordeal, followed by a late night at the hospital, that you didn't sleep in. You look a little tired."

"I can sleep in tomorrow. Today I want to be with everyone I love."

Mom stood up and lifted Harper down from the table. She told her to go find Daddy, then turned to look at me. "Are you feeling okay? You seem…" She frowned and then looked me in the eye.

I didn't answer, but somehow she knew. I could see it in her eyes. I placed a hand on my stomach. "How'd you know? I only just began to suspect myself. I haven't even taken a test yet."

Mom smiled. "A mother always knows."

"Please don't say anything. It's too early. After last time I want to be sure things are going to work out. If I am pregnant my plan is not to say anything for at least a month, maybe even two. I don't want to disappoint Zak again."

"He won't be disappointed. He loves you. He wants to be there for you no matter what happens."

"I know, but I think it will be better that way."

Mom pulled me into her arms and hugged me tight. "I understand your hesitation and I promise not to say anything, but I think things are going to work out this time."

I laid my head on Mom's shoulder and suppressed a tiny smile. I really, really hoped she was right.

Up Next in the Zoe and Lani Crossover Event

Zak and Zoe head to Maui to help Luke and Lani track down a hacker and find the truth behind a murder.

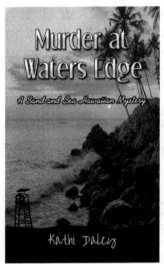

Preorder today:
http://amzn.to/2nbib6A

Recipes

Recipes from Kathi

Salmon Wheels
Crab and Artichoke Dip
Potato Salad
Fudge Sundae Pie

Recipes from Readers

Meatball Cranberry Appetizer—submitted
by Sharon Guagliardo
Key Lime Cake—submitted by Patty Liu
Bohemian Coffee Cake—submitted by Pam
Curran
Boiled Shrimp—submitted by Nancy Farris

Salmon Wheels

1 can (14 oz. approx.) salmon, drained,
bones and skin removed
1 pkg. (8 oz.) cream cheese, softened
4 tbs. salsa
2 tbs. parsley
8 flour tortillas

In small bowl, combine salmon, cream
cheese, salsa, and parsley. Spread about 2
tbs. onto each tortilla. Roll each tortilla
tight. Wrap in plastic wrap. Refrigerate 2–
3 hours. Slice each tortilla into bite-size
pieces.

Crab and Artichoke Dip

8 oz. cream cheese, softened
8 oz. Havarti cheese, grated
2 cans (approx. 14 oz. each) artichoke hearts, diced
8 oz. crabmeat, fresh or canned
2 cups Parmesan cheese, grated
1 cup sour cream
2 tsp. horseradish (add more if you like it hot)

Mix and bake at 450 degrees for 30–45 minutes; stir after 20 minutes.

Serve with baguette slices, tortilla chips, or crackers.

Potato Salad

6 medium potatoes, boiled and skinned (Boil in skin until very done. When skin begins to crack, rinse with cool water and then peel skin away; it should peel very easily.)
8 hardboiled eggs (I sometimes use up to 12)
2 cups mayonnaise
1 cup hot dog relish (yellow)

Combine in large bowl. Season to taste. I use Lawry's salt, pepper, and paprika.

Fudge Sundae Pie

Crust:
¼ cup light corn syrup
2 tbs. brown sugar
3 tbs. butter
2½ cups Rice Krispies cereal

Combine corn syrup, brown sugar, and butter in saucepan. Cook over medium heat until it boils. Pour over Rice Krispies. Stir together and then press into buttered pie plate.

Topping:
½ cup peanut butter
½ cup chocolate fudge sauce
3 tbs. corn syrup
(Note: I often make extra topping and pile it on thick. It's up to you.)

Mix together and spread half on piecrust. Layer in softened ice cream. I use vanilla, but coffee or chocolate works as well. Spread other half of topping over top.

Freeze for 2–3 hours.

Meatball Cranberry Appetizer

Submitted by Sharon Guagliardo

Had these at a friend's house for someone's birthday. They were really good.

1 can (14 oz.) whole berry cranberry sauce
1 can (14 oz.) sauerkraut, rinsed and well drained
1 bottle (12 oz.) chili sauce
¾ cup packed brown sugar
1 pkg. (32 oz.) frozen fully cooked home-style meatballs, thawed

In a 4-qt. slow cooker, combine the cranberry sauce, sauerkraut, chili sauce, and brown sugar. Stir in meatballs. Cover and cook on low 4–5 hours or until heated through.

Makes about 5 dozen.

Key Lime Cake

Submitted by Patty Liu

Cake:

1 box lemon cake mix
1 pkg. (4-serving size) Jell-O Instant
Lemon Pudding Mix
4 eggs
1 cup vegetable oil
¾ cup water
¼ cup key lime juice (Key West Key Lime
Juice or whatever's available)

Glaze:
2 cups confectioner's sugar
⅓ cup key lime juice
2 tbs. cold water
3 tbs. butter

Preheat oven to 350 degrees. Combine
cake and pudding mixes, eggs, oil, water,
and ¼ cup key lime juice in a large bowl.
Beat at medium speed with electric mixer
for 2 minutes. Pour into a 10-in. tube cake
pan; bake 50–60 minutes or until a cake

tester in center comes out clean; cool in pan 25 minutes. After cooling shake to ensure cake is loose in pan; generously poke holes in warm cake with a long-tined fork.

For glaze, combine confectioner's sugar, ⅓ cup key lime juice, water, and melted butter in a medium bowl. Beat with mixer till smooth; pour slowly over top of cake; cool completely in pan. Invert onto serving plate and dust with confectioner's sugar.

Tip: Fresh, frozen and thawed, or bottled lime juice may be substituted for key lime juice.

Bohemian Coffee Cake

Submitted by Pam Curran

1 cup vegetable oil
1 cup light brown sugar
1 cup sugar
1 cup buttermilk
2 eggs
2½ cups flour
1 tsp. salt
1 tsp. baking powder
1 tsp. nutmeg
1 tsp. cinnamon
1 tsp. baking soda
1 tsp. vanilla
1 cup coconut
1 or 2 cups chopped pecans

Mix together all the above ingredients in the order listed. Bake at 350 degrees for about 1 hour. This can be made as a 3 layer or a sheet cake.

Icing:

1 4-oz. pkg. cream cheese

1 box powdered sugar
About ½ stick margarine
1 or 2 cups chopped pecans
2 tsp. vanilla

Mix together and spread on cooled cake. If desired, you can double the icing amount.

Boiled Shrimp

Submitted by Nancy Farris

One of our favorite weeknight meals. It's really good and it's really easy and quick!

1 lb. large shrimp, peeled and deveined
12 large pimento-stuffed olives, quartered lengthwise
8 oz. cherry or grape tomatoes, cut in half lengthwise
2 cloves garlic, minced
1 tbs. thyme, fresh or dried
1 tsp. salt
1 lemon, juiced
4 tbs. olive oil

Preheat broiler.

Put all ingredients into large bowl and toss thoroughly. Place in large, ovenproof baking dish. Place under broiler for 5 minutes. Remove and stir so that any uncooked shrimp will be exposed. Place

back under broiler for another 3–4
minutes until shrimp are cooked.

Serve in the baking dish with a loaf of
crusty bread for dipping.

Serves 2

Books by Kathi Daley

Come for the murder, stay for the romance.

Zoe Donovan Cozy Mystery:
Halloween Hijinks
The Trouble With Turkeys
Christmas Crazy
Cupid's Curse
Big Bunny Bump-off
Beach Blanket Barbie
Maui Madness
Derby Divas
Haunted Hamlet
Turkeys, Tuxes, and Tabbies
Christmas Cozy
Alaskan Alliance
Matrimony Meltdown
Soul Surrender
Heavenly Honeymoon
Hopscotch Homicide
Ghostly Graveyard
Santa Sleuth
Shamrock Shenanigans
Kitten Kaboodle
Costume Catastrophe

Candy Cane Caper
Holiday Hangover
Easter Escapade
Camp Carter – *July 2017*

Zimmerman Academy The New Normal
Ashton Falls Cozy Cookbook

Tj Jensen Paradise Lake Mysteries by Henery Press

Pumpkins in Paradise
Snowmen in Paradise
Bikinis in Paradise
Christmas in Paradise
Puppies in Paradise
Halloween in Paradise
Treasure in Paradise – *April 2017*
Fireworks in Paradise – *October 2017*

Whales and Tails Cozy Mystery:

Romeow and Juliet
The Mad Catter
Grimm's Furry Tail
Much Ado About Felines
Legend of Tabby Hollow
Cat of Christmas Past
A Tale of Two Tabbies
The Great Catsby
Count Catula
The Cat of Christmas Present
A Winter's Tail
The Taming of the Tabby – *June 2017*

Seacliff High Mystery:

The Secret
The Curse
The Relic
The Conspiracy
The Grudge
The Shadow – *June 2017*

Sand and Sea Hawaiian Mystery:

Murder at Dolphin Bay
Murder at Sunrise Beach
Murder at the Witching Hour

Murder at Christmas
Murder at Turtle Cove
Murder at Water's Edge – *May 2017*

Road to Christmas Romance:
Road to Christmas Past

Writer's Retreat Southern Mystery:
First Case – *May 2017*
Second Look – *July 2017*

Kathi Daley lives with her husband, kids, grandkids, and Bernese mountain dogs in beautiful Lake Tahoe. When she isn't writing, she likes to read (preferably at the beach or by the fire), cook (preferably something with chocolate or cheese), and garden (planting and planning, not weeding). She also enjoys spending time on the water when she's not hiking, biking, or snowshoeing the miles of desolate trails surrounding her home.

Kathi uses the mountain setting in which she lives, along with the animals (wild and domestic) that share her home, as inspiration for her cozy mysteries.

Kathi is a top 100 mystery writer for Amazon and won the 2014 award for both Best Cozy Mystery Author and Best Cozy Mystery Series.

She currently writes six series: Zoe Donovan Cozy Mysteries, Whales and Tails Island Mysteries, Sand and Sea Hawaiian Mysteries, Tj Jensen Paradise Lake Mysteries, Writer's Retreat Southern Mysteries, and Seacliff High Teen Mysteries.

Giveaway:

I do a giveaway for books, swag, and gift cards every week in my newsletter, *The Daley Weekly* **http://eepurl.com/NRPDf**

Other links to check out:

Kathi Daley Blog – publishes each Friday **http://kathidaleyblog.com**

Webpage – **www.kathidaley.com**

Facebook at Kathi Daley Books – **www.facebook.com/kathidaleybooks**

Kathi Daley Teen – **www.facebook.com/kathidaleyteen**

Kathi Daley Books Group Page – **https://www.facebook.com/groups/569578823146850/**

E-mail – **kathidaley@kathidaley.com**

Goodreads – **https://www.goodreads.com/author/show/7278377.Kathi_Daley**

Twitter at Kathi Daley@kathidaley – **https://twitter.com/kathidaley**

Amazon Author Page – **https://www.amazon.com/author/kathidaley**

BookBub – **https://www.bookbub.com/authors/kathi-daley**

Pinterest – **http://www.pinterest.com/kathidaley/**

CPSIA information can be obtained
at www.ICGtesting.com
Printed in the USA
BVHW040826190320
575431BV00007B/158

9 781543 299724